IN TOO DEEP

A Novel by Paris Iman

In Too Deep Copyright © 2021 Paris Iman

ISBN 13: 978-1-7354589-1-5

First Printing February 2021
Printed in the United States of America

This is a work of fiction. Any references or similarities to actual events, real people, living, or dead, or to real locales are intended to give the novel a sense of reality. Any similarity in other names, characters, places, and incidents is entirely coincidental.

CONTACT THE AUTHOR

INSTAGRAM
@parisiman_

Email Me
info@parisman.com

AMAZON
www.amazon.com/author/ParisIman

DEDICATION

To my ladies,
I want to see you win.
Period.
Never love someone so much you lose yourself, only to find out in the
end what you thought was real love was just a game.
Be happy alone, don't be so hard on yourself.
A woman's intuition speaks, don't overlook that shit.
I no longer want to see you hurting or lacking.
I want to witness you getting everything you deserve.
This is dedicated to you.

PREFACE

This pussy will have your boyfriend single, baby father babyless and husband asking for a divorce. I'm not saying this with pride, I'm just stating facts.

A nigga will fuck you today and fuck another bitch today. Thought I was going to say tomorrow? Nope bitch, TODAY!

They are VICIOUS!

Sex has made me do some dumb things over the years, including ending up in relationships because I got attached. It would be so mind blowing that I couldn't give that sweet D up. Often times, still despite knowing the relationships would never work, my heart was broken. Eventually the logical side of my brain won the battle though and I began to cut these niggas lose left to right.

I've been through hell, numerous flings, run-ins with the law, heated arguments, and more than a few knock-outs, I've played the role of both the side-chick and the trap queen only to realize I have an addiction that I somehow can't seem to shake.

We see it all the time: ladies love outlaws, and good girls cannot resist bad boys.

But there's so much that comes with these "bad boys".

Every nigga goin' teach you something...

He either goin' teach you how a lady is supposed to be treated, or how the game is supposed to be played.

After twenty-five years, I've learned that dick ain't worth it if it disrupts your peace. Ladies, if your man is trash, I encourage you to get better dick, positive dick, loving dick, a dick that'll cherish only you sis.

Young and naive, trapped in games of lies and deception, I now know the true meaning of "everything that glitters ain't gold."

Oh yeah, by the way, my name is Parker, and this is my story.

PARKER'S PLAYLIST

1. Keyshia Cole x Vault
2. Keri Hilson x Where Did He Go
3. NBA YoungBoy x Valuable Pain
4. Jhene Aiko x Triggered
5. Jhene Aiko x Above and Beyond
6. Jhene Aiko x Pray for You
7. Tink x Bonnie & Clyde
8. Tink x Treat me Like Somebody
9. Tink x Stuck
10. Tink x Hopeless Romantic
11. Summer Walker x Let It Go
12. Summer Walker x I'll Kill You
13. Summer Walker x Nobody Else
14. Summer Walker x Off of You
15. Future | Young Thug x Real Love
16. 42 Dugg x Ride wit Me
17. Lil Baby x Emotionally Scarred
18. Monica x Why Her
19. Heather Headly x In My Mind
20. Tamia x Still
21. Mary J Blige x Stay Down
22. Mary J Blige x Hurt Again
23. Rihanna x We Ride
24. Rihanna x Ps. I'm Still Not Over You
25. Beyonce x Yes
26. Destiny's Child x IF
27. Nivea x Complicated
28. Ciara x I Found Myself
29. Ciara x My Love
30. Rod Wave x Titanic

SIGNIFICANT TERMS

HEARTBREAK
Overwhelming distress, deeply sorrowful.

ABANDONMENT
Having been deserted or cast off.

DEPRESSION
mental health disorder characterized by persistently depressed mood or loss of interest in activities causing significant impairment in daily life.

LOVE
an intense feeling of deep affection.

DESIRE
a strong feeling of wanting to have something or wishing for something to happen.

SELF-LOVE
regard for one's own well-being and happiness

SELF-ESTEEM
confidence in one's own worth or abilities.

TOXICITY
very harmful or unpleasant in a persuasive or insidious way.

LETS BE REAL

The only people who are fools are the ones who go through life and don't learn shit!

Anything you go through you are meant to learn something from it!

We gotta realize it comes to a point where it ain't even them hurting us, we're hurting ourselves.

We know the shit they do and we go along with it.

We speak on it and stay.

They do the same thing.

We know what kind of people we date, and we still date them anyway.

Then wanna cry about it.

That's like tie'n our shoestrings together trying to run knowing we gonna get fucked up.

But we just wanna be a damn dummy.

Forreal, it's like we gotta make sense so if we goin' date them kind of people we gotta be able to control our feelings cause if not we gonna be sad as shit.

We set ourselves up, we know right from wrong.

We know what we deserve,

Yet we settle for the basics.

And the thing is, we not stupid!

Bitches be having gut feelings before they actually even step out.

We just let it happen.

Woman intuition speaks, stop overlooking that shit…

JOURNAL ENTRY #1

Why do I keep choosing different dudes with the same concept?
Why is it that I leave one bad situation and walk myself right into another one?
And why do I go from one bad dude to another one?
It's a continuous cycle.

SAME NIGGA, DIFFERENT CONCEPT

It happens all the time, without fail. The sweetest girl goes for that terrible worthless bad boy - AGAIN! She has so much to offer, the perfect catch, yet she chooses a boy (we can't even bear to call him a man) a handful of notches below her level.

It isn't usually a one-time slip up, but some type of pattern that repeats itself - one jerk after another, always resulting with a broken heart and a swollen face full of mascara infused tears.

What could possibly cause a beautiful, well rounded, bright-futured female to stoop to the levels of an unaccomplished unqualified bad boy, that would treat her nothing even remotely close to what she is worth?

Every woman has had a friend who dated a guy who was clearly bad news, but she just couldn't resist. Maybe, that "friend" was you. And yet, despite all the warnings and red flags, the pull of dating a "bad boy" was just too strong. So, even with all of the signs that heartbreak is on the horizon, why do we still find bad boys so appealing?

In the most extreme and negative interpretation, bad guys display qualities of the so-called psychological dark triad.

And yet, sometimes we just can't quit them.

Bad boys" free us from the pressure of being "good girls."

"Girls possess a range of traits, like rebelliousness.

These traits are typically repressed during childhood, as females are socialized to be compliant and agreeable. If a girl's inner life is unexpressed, she may be drawn to a bad boy as a way of vicariously expressing her own inner rebel."

12

Basically, "We're attracted to qualities in others that we ourselves wish we had,"

A 'good girl' may admire the bad boy's sense of freedom. Despite the fact that this quality makes him an unsuitable partner for the long-term, it can make him so attractive, it's seemingly worth the potential pain associated."

When we want something, we can't or shouldn't have, our desire for it grows exponentially.

INTRODUCTION

The Night before Court

Parker let tears fall from her eyes and she tried to both maneuver her car and wipe snot from her running nose. Her emotions had gotten the best of her and they were spiraling out of control. She felt like she was losing herself.

The rain hit the ground hard and her windows even harder. The skies were overhung with blankets of grey, so much that she could barely tell the difference between the sky and the clouds. The rain usually calmed her but tonight she was on edge. The road became alive with more splashes than her eyes could appreciate. But yet together, it all brought a soothing sound, a natural melody.

Parker continued to cry and sulk as she made her way to her grandmother's house. No matter the age, she learned a lot of lessons from the seasoned member. She wiped crumbs off of her face and had given her treats for as long as she could remember. She carried inside her a tank that was always full of love. Her eyes lit up and she always extended her arms whenever they saw each other.

Bearing to her right at about 40 mph Parker sped down the street and quickly pulled up on the curb and hopped out her car. She scrambled to her feet as she reached the door. Frantically crying and beginning to get soaked she hit the doorbell several times before Janette showed up.

"My God, baby what's going on? What's the matter?" Janette asked concerned.

"Grandma I had nowhere else to go, I had no one else to talk to." Parker confessed and she sobbed.

"Well, what about baby?" she wiped Parker's face and consoled her.

"I just can't seem to forget and forgive and it's eating me up. It's tearing me down. I don't know what to do or how to fix it." Parker cried.

Grandparents were accepted as honorable and wise. They were expected to know the answers to all the questions and be fair in their judgements, and so she was. She removed Parker's coat and wet clothing and grabbed a blanket to wrap around her. She guided Parker to the couch, and they continued their conversation.

"The best revenge is to be unlike him who performed the injury. If you spend your time hoping someone will suffer the consequences for what they did to your heart, then you're allowing them to hurt you a second time in your mind baby." She held Parker and let her cry in her arms. "Grudges are for those who insist that they are owed something. They don't owe you anything Parker! Karma! Karma comes after everyone eventually. You can't get away with screwing people over, it doesn't matter who you are. What goes around comes around. That's how it works. Sooner or later the universe will serve the revenge that they deserve. " She paused and rubbed Parker's back. This had been the first she had ever seen Parker break down.
"Throughout life Parker, people will make you mad, disrespect you and treat you bad. Let God deal with them baby, because hate in your heart will consume you too. Not forgiving is like drinking rat poison and then waiting for the rat to die. Revenge is not sweet baby; it's gloomy. The weak can never forgive. Forgiveness is the attribute of the strong! The truth is, unless you let go, unless you forgive yourself, unless you forgive whatever situation, unless you realize that the situation is over, YOU cannot move forward. Forgiveness isn't approving what happened, it's choosing to rise above it!" she squeezed Parker in her embrace, she spoke with so much confidence and exuded an abundance of wisdom. Her words were soothing.

16

Precinct, Interrogation January 2021

The walls provided a high degree of soundproofing. The doors were windowless and flushed with metal and solid cores. There was a solid gypsum board ceiling and only three pieces of furniture; a table, a chair for Parker and a chair for the Detective.

Back in college Parker studied Criminal Law, she knew from the jump interrogations were designed to produce confessions and the best way to protect herself was to not make a statement without her lawyer present. In fact, she knew not to say anything at all.

"You have all the motive in the world." The Detective paced the tiny room back and forth. He grinned and shook his head in hopes of intimidating Parker, but she didn't budge. In fact, she was stuck.

"Can you picture the headlines in the media? I mean, I wonder what they'll call it." he continued to joke. Things had gotten pretty bad, but she didn't want him dead. Apart of her had been relieved, but she was still hurting.

"And the girl, Ivory. Can you tell me what she has to do with all of this?" The Detective stopped pacing and stood there with a puzzled look on his face. Seconds later he began to grin and started pacing again.

Fuck that bitch, she got everything she deserved.

Court, Sentencing February 2021

The enclosed space of the courtroom gave Parker an uneasy feeling. She hated court, she hated anything that dealt with the criminal justice system in general. The seats were hard, and the scent of moth balls filled her nostrils. Each step of the trial process was a part of a rigorous system driven by a single purpose; to protect the rights of citizens by resolving

disputes fairly. Parker's trial moved forward quickly once the prosecutor presented his case. The judge came to a verdict. "What is obvious to this court is that you're in need of professional help and anger management counseling. This court is suggesting you seek counseling. I am requiring it as a part of your stay out of jail." The judge demanded.
"Do I make myself clear?"
Parker sighed and responded. "Yes, your honor. "

Present Day January 2021, Therapy Session
Parker put off seeing a therapist for years. It wasn't that she was against therapy, in fact, she merrily recommended it to friends going through a rough time, but for some reason, she just had never been ready to take that leap; until today. She wasn't ready to be vulnerable, or expressive, and explore her inner challenges and deal with problems that many keep to themselves. Instead, she was here, sitting with a trained professional to guide her through.
"Yea I wanted his ass dead but I ain't kill him." Parker shrugged her shoulders and crossed her legs as she sat across from her new therapist, Ada Hines. She was a slim woman who stood about 5'9. She had to be pushing sixty and the kinky twists in her hair had to be more than three months old.
"Before we talk about his death let's start from the beginning.." Ada began.
"It was great in the beginning." Parker cut her off and started to reminisce. "He was everything, or so I thought."
"And then?" Ada questioned.
"And then shit took a turn for the worse! What do you mean "and then?" Parker whinnied dramatically. "And then he tried to fuckin kill me. But would you like me to give you a

timeline Ma'am? Is that what you want? Chronological events? I can give you that."

Ada was taken aback but she let Parker express herself.

"Okay so where would you like to start?"

Parker leaned back in her chair, crossed her legs and folded her arms.

"Can I smoke in here Mrs. Ada Therapy lady please?" Parker asked bluntly. Before her session she made sure to roll up something nice. She figured why not have a session during a session.

"Uh, sure." Afraid of the aftermath she went against her better judgement and let Parker light her blunt.

"Nothing was the same after February. Nothing got better, it got worse. I was miserable, I was so depressed and drained. I lost so much weight and my hair started falling out it was just a hot ass mess. But I found my way out. " Parker let a tear fall.

"What caused that?" Ada wanted to know more.

She shrugged. "I guess we'll start from the beginning then." Parker grinned.

CHAPTER 1

TOXCITY

"Marquee"

JOURNAL ENTRY #2

The same person I bent over backwards for. The same person I once loved to the moon and back, he tried to kill me. Like how is this possible? It was sooo good then it got sooooo bad. I gave him my last, I provided for him, I gave him a place to stay, and now you go to extreme measures to have me killed? It's beyond me but it's fuckin wit me cus I had so much love for that boy.

P

"I want to love myself more, where do I start?" The truth is
you have to start with yourself, it's that simple. Be
accountable and realize if you want shit to be different, you
have to take a leap of faith and start doing things differently
with no regrets.

September 2019
Parker speed walked down the sidewalk as she eyed her fresh manicured feet. She touched her baby hairs that rested on her forehead and ran her hands thru her ponytail.

"Bitch come on!" Reema screeched with Parker on her heels.

"The GPS say ten minutes."

"Girl okay, we goin get there." Parker rolled her eyes and hopped in her 2018 Honda coupe with an attitude.

"Okay well I need to smoke." She was accompanied by Reema, a high school associate, and they were on their way to feed their habit. Parker dipped and dabbed in a few drugs when she went away to college but back at home her choice of drug was strictly weed.

"Bitch, I can't wait to see that nigga Quee." Reema sat in the passenger seat of Parker's Honda and blushed as she twiddled her fingers. "He looks so fuckin good." Reema licked her lips and tucked her stiff hair behind her ears. She was so unattractive, her breast were huge and her ass was super flat, sad to say she was shaped like a wet sponge. Not to mention her previous relationship had taken a turn for the worse and left her with four missing teeth in the front and veneers.

Parker shook her head. "I know you ain't talkin' bout that nigga Quee from high school bitch."

"I sure am." Reema assured. "It's the dick for me." She bragged.

"Aww you fucked him?" Parker put the car in cruise and soaked up this juicy tea.

"Girl yes! That shit was magnificent, and I want more." She stated.

Parker burst into laughter as she glanced at Reema from time to time in the passenger seat. The crop top she wore barely fit, and her feet hung out of her Payless sandals. The jean jeggings hugged her so tight Parker had no idea how she got them buttoned up. Reema's shoulders were broad, and her back was wide.

"Mm that's tea." Parker giggled.

"Girl that shit is old." Reema waved her hands in the air.

"That man fresh out, five-year bid, he looks good."

"Oh yea, wat he was in for?"

"Girl some shit from back in high school that had to do with Aiden."

"Word."

Quee was that nigga back in high school. Parker sat back and wondered what all the hype was about now.

**

Parker backed into the nearest parking spot and watched the clear bubbles light up on Reema phone as they waited for a response.

"Oh, fuck no P, go get it. He got his dog with him." Parker turned her face up and exited the car.

This bitch really throwin me off. Parker slammed the door, as she turned around Quee was standing right before her. Struck by his beauty and unique physique, Parker let her mouth hang open for a few seconds before she caught herself. Quee was 6'3 and tatted from head to toe. His broad shoulders stuck out as the wife beater cling to his chest.

"Wassup Parker." Quee shuffled from side to side as he filled Parker out. A lot had changed since high school. Parker's ponytail fell down her back, her bubble eyes were alluring. Her nose ring glistened in the sun as she turned her head to get a better look at Quee.

"Wow." She whispered as she looked him up and down. "It's been a while, how are you?"

"I mean it feels good to be home." He continued to fill her out.

"That's wassup." with not much to say they both stood in silence and took in each other's features. Back in high school they flirted from time to time, but it was nothing serious in Parker's eyes and besides she felt they were too young, but she finally got a chance to see what the hype was about, and boy was she impressed.

"Damn it's been a minute though, you look good." Quee flashed his pearly white teeth.

"Yea likewise."

October 2019
As the weeks went by Parker was head over heels. She was seeing Marquee on the regular. The talked throughout the day and as far as she knew he was outside getting some money when he wasn't with her, or so she thought.

Parker threw on her Classic Milano di Rouge Hunter green two-piece sweatsuit which she paired with her black and white retro 1's. She switched bags and decided to sport her Marc Jacobs Fanny pack around her waist. Her hair had been pulled back into a sleek ponytail parted in the middle, Su Young had waxed her eyebrows to perfection and her nose ring shinned.

She sauntered out of the house and hopped in Marquee's passenger seat. He never mentioned where they were going, he texted her 20mins prior and told her to be ready and that was that. Parker found him to be so demanding and dominant; she loved that shit.

Marquee was your average Maryland nigga. He was born in Southern Maryland, raised by parents in Clinton, which was located in PG County and he never really stepped foot into the city until high school. Although he didn't live in a big house with both parents, he was still a spoiled brat who was born with a silver spoon in his mouth.

Marquee had a long rap sheet. From attempted murder to robbery, he was never behind bars for one thing. He was a petty criminal with a reckless mindset. He made moves before he calculated them therefore causing his to pay consequences here and there. Back in 2014 right after graduation, he tagged along with one of his main men and murdered someone. Word on the street is that he snitched and got his sentence reduced but no one could find proof so that rumor was laid to rest.

Marquee maneuvered through traffic like a pro as he headed downtown. In no time they arrived at their destination. Parker was amazed at the views. She had been down Georgetown a few times but only to shop. The area was surrounded with Federal style architecture, cobblestone streets and fashion and design shops. The dining scene was defined by upmarket restaurants and waterfront seafood spots. While the park had a riverside and gardens along the canal. It was beautiful.

The valet opened their doors and Marquee escorted Parker inside Sequoia. The newly renovated restaurant was located on the waterfront right along the banks of the Potomac River. The vast floor-to-ceiling windows offered Magnificent views and the interior design was absolutely amazing as the surroundings.

"Oh, he a fancy ass jailbird"

This was new to Parker. She was so used to the bare fuckin minimum she had never gotten courted properly. It was always *"pull up on me"* or *"come see me"* never *"be ready in 20 I'll let you know when I'm outside"*. This was different and she loved every minute of it.

**

He sure did know how to put on a facade.

"This nigga acting like he so top tier, still living with his damn momma in this funky ass house"

As Parker entered the home the stench of hot dog piss filled her nostrils. Roaches crawled into hiding as they made their way up the steps. Parker was disgusted to a certain extent. She pushed the negative thoughts to the back of her mind.

"I guess I can give him a pass, I mean, I did sleep on an air mattress with Quis when he had mice so I guess that's equivalent."

The house was by far a hot trifling mess. Clothes were strewn all over the place, the smell of dirty dishes lingered in the air and little droppings of dog shit had been scattered across the floor. Parker figured they were having some plumbing issues as well when she took note of the missing ceiling above the dining room. Still slightly holding her breath she descended into the basement following behind Marquee.

Parker began to talk so much shit in her head.

"I'm tryin figure out why this nigga got this big ass bed and this little bit of space, you can barely move in this motherfucka"

**

The sex was somewhat amazing, but the experience had been rather horrible. To make matters worse Juanita charged through the door like a mad man bright and early while Parker was half naked.

"Oh unt! Fuck no!" Judy burst through the door shouting shaking her head from side to side waving her hands in the air. "I ain't goin keep tellin' you to stop bringin' all these fast ass girls up in my got damn house!"

Judy was not the prettiest thing walking at all, in fact she was far from average. If I was a man I wouldn't dare look her way. She favored Marquee in so many ways, she had strong facial features. Her teeth were rotten in the front, her hair never stayed done and when she did attempt to get it styled, her tracks were both stiff noticeable. She was short and

27

chunky, round like a ball. Her stomach stick out and she never wore clothes that fit so her stretch marks and rolls showed themselves often.

Startled by all the commotion Parker jumped up exposing g her naked body as did Marquee. He slid out of bed with his manhood swinging from left to right.

"Aye man get the fuck on wit all dat goofy shit Ma, no funny."

With one eye open he palmed her face and mushed her backwards causing her to stumble as he slammed the door in her face.

In the midst of all the chaos Parker had been scrambling trying to dress herself but she was distracted by a mother roach that had found its way into the bed.

"This dirty mutherfucka! I gotta get the fuck outta here right now! This shit is absurd!"

Judy continued with her rant which infuriated Marquee. He was both embarrassed and annoyed.

"Man this bitch bout to piss me off!"

Marquee threw on his drawls and stormed out in a frenzy causing a loud thud. Parker jumped up and screeched at the family of roaches that slid down the wall once he shut the door behind him.

"Oh my god, it's so many of them!"

January 2020

"You need to get a fuckin job! Keep sitting around thinkin' your shit goin take off and you don't even have the money to fund that shit!" Marquee paced the room back and forth as he taunted Parker.

Months had gone by and they were both still in the same boat, but Marquee felt the need to point it out. Neither one of them were working; Parker had an entrepreneur mindset while Marquee wanted to hustle his way to the top. Everything had been all peaches and cream until Marquee began to show his true colors. He was changing everyday right before her eyes, yet she still had been willing to make things work despite their differences and the strain on the relationship.

Parker sat on the floor with tears in her eyes as Marquee tore her apart with his words.

"You aint shit forreal and iont wanna be wit nobody that ain't got nothing goin for herself." Marquee folded his arms and mugged on Parker.

It usually took some time, but Parker knew her worth deep down inside. She let Marquee slide majority of the time, but she popped her shit back often.

"Nothing goin' for myself?" She mocked him.

"Yea Moe you broke as shit" he spat back standing over top of her.

Parker burst into laughter "Is that a joke?"

Parker was a very private person, there was so much she didn't show and tell, like her money. However. that had been the least of her worries, it was his audacity.

"Nigga fuck you, your penny pinching ass! You ain't shit either! You sell that dirt ass weed, make a lil profit and think you a fuckin kingpin? Try again my man."

The room had been split into two. Marquee occupied one side as did Parker. Her grandmother allowed him to move in due to his circumstances at home. Marquee paced his side back and forth and began to pack his belongings. Parker dropped her mouth in both amazement and disbelief.

"What the fuck are you doing?"

"I'm leaving. I don't want to be with you. Go find a job instead of tryin sit up under me all day." Marquee was calm but agitated.

"Are you serious right now?" Parker's heart sank. Apart of her was slightly relieved but the half of her was hurt to her core. She became not only emotionally dependent but attached as well. She was afraid to be alone. She didn't know herself anymore. Reading was foreign to her as was writing; her favorite. She had been avoiding her friends and became very distant. Her social life had gone to shit when she granted Marquee the wish of driving her vehicle, she was in the house 24/7.

"Marquee are you serious?" Parker shunned and grabbed his arms as he attempted to depart. "Can we talk about this please" she pleaded.

"Ain't nothing to talk about Parker have a nice life." He snatched away and descended down the stairs with Parker on his heels begging him to stay.

And just like that he was gone.

Later that night

The night was still young, so Marquee decided to go joyriding with an old friend. He sat in the passenger seat and lit his blunt.

"So, you single now huh bruh?" Juju joked.

Marquee and Juju grew up together back in the day. She was his ride or die and just as gay as they come.

"Man fuck that bitch she really give a nigga a headache" Marquee confessed.

Lil Durk blared through the speakers and the two just vibed as they dipped in and out of traffic. Startled by the red and blue lights, Juju dropped the blunt and put her car in sport.

Marquee shook his head as his heart started to race. He was fresh out and the last thing he wanted was to go back in. "Bruh pull over, we ain't got shit but weed." Marquee demanded and so she did. Juju slowed the car down and pulled over in Sussex square in Forestville. Because she put on a chase about five cars had pulled behind her. "Fuck!" she shouted and banged on the wheel.

Officers approached both sides of the vehicle with their hands on their holsters ready to fire their weapons.

"I need you both to exit the vehicle" an officer demanded in an unfriendly tone. "Now!"

Marquee eased his way out the car along with Juju while the officers forced their doors opened. They were forcefully pinned to the car, searched and asked several questions.

"Your tags are suspended, and you attempted to flee from the police, what's goin on tonight guys?" The officer teased while the others searched juju car.

"Look at what we got." The second officer threw four bags of Marquee's weed in the air.

"Jackpot!" The third officer rose from the car with a Glock in his hand.

"Oh, iont know who that belong to." Juju lied.

Marquee dropped his head. He knew that shit belonged to Juju and it just wasn't sitting right with him that she wasn't owning up to the gun being hers. On top of the he had no idea she was carrying.

The last thing he wanted to do was run but he felt he had no choice, it was either that or go back to prison. To make matters worse he was already on probation and skating in thin ice with Juanita, so he had no idea who to call.

Before they could read them their Miranda rights Marquee took off running. He was gone in no time, but they still had Juju.

31

**

It had been exactly 9hrs and 56 mins since they had split. It had rained that night, so she lit a candle and opened her windows. Parker laid in bed and listened to Ashanti until she drifted off.

Not quite in a deep sleep she jumped at the vibration of her phone. It was an unknown number, so she ignored it. It wasn't until she got a call from Juanita, that got her attention. Although she dreaded conversation and faking a liking toward her, Parker answered.

"Hey miss Juanita."

There was silence for a few seconds.

"Boo, it's me, I need you to come get me." Irritated but excited to hear his voice Parker instantly caught butterflies.

"Ha this nigga just tried to cut ties with me now he need my ass, tuh pathetic!"

"Wtf happened Marquee and where you at?"

"Man, some shìt went down wit Juju, she wasn't tryin' take her charge and shìt and I ran."

Parker laid in bed and cackled while he was on mute.

"He gotta be the dumbest motherfucker."

"Why did you run Marquee?" Parker questioned.

"Cause she had a gun, I'm already ready on probation and shìt!" He shouted. "Can you come get me please. "Marquee pleaded.

"Yea I'm on my way." Parker responded without hesitation.

February 20th, 2020

"He trifling Parker! He ain't shit! Ole ungrateful ass!" Parker sat on the phone with Judy while she vented and expressed her frustrations with her child. "I brought his ass in this world and I'll take that motherfucka right out. I can't believe I gave birth to such a selfish spiteful child!" Parker and Judy's relationship had strengthened over the months but Parker still wasn't too fond of her. She knew deep down inside Judy held a strong disliking to her and she couldn't figure out why. She talked about Parker behind her back and said the utmost horrible things about her. Despite their issues, Parker kept it cute and respectful for Marquee. Besides, her mother didn't raise her like that.

"He so fuckin disrespectful! Now why would you bite the hand that feeds you?" She continued.

Parker sat in deep thought as she listened to Judy rant. She couldn't argue or deny a word she had said. Marquee was definitely all for self and still she stayed around in hopes things would change, but, they never did. Every day she figured the relationship would get better but it didn't, if anything it would get worse. As much as Marquee pushed her out she forced herself in. He was distant, rude and uninterested and Parker was so weak minded.

"Parker iont know how you do that shit, that lil motherfucka make me sick!"

Parker shook herself out of her thoughts, alarmed by the several dings on her phone she tuned Judy out. Her heart dropped. She was both confused and shocked, but more so upset; she wanted blood. Parker opened her Instagram app and skimmed through the messages that were sent to her.

"Miss you lil Ma"

"I miss you too Luv"

"Can't wait to get back in dat"

"And I can't wait either.. hurry up."

"I'm getting out the shower now, I'm goin hit you when I leave out."

"iight.."

Parker's anxiety immediately flared up, sweat particles formed and after a few seconds she was drenched. Her hands started to shake and she saw nothing but red. Without hesitation she dropped the phone and emerged from the car. Galloping to the front door she charged up the steps. She heard the water running and figured he must have still been in the shower.

"Perfect! Ima beat this bitch like he stole something! Cus he really got me fucked up!"

Parker gently eased into her room. She went directly to her top drawer where she kept her belts and pulled out her shinny leather black one. She was tired, embarrassed, hurt but more so stressed.

Before he had a chance to cut the water off Parker burst through the door on 10! She snatched the curtains back, raise her hand and tore Marquee up. He twisted, turned and slipped while in the shower as he tried to get a hold on the belt.

"Bruh wtf is you doin Moe! Parker! Chill the fuck out!"

She continued to slap his butter bald naked ass with her belt until she was ready to stop!

"Play wit somebody else pussy! You got me fucked up!"

"What the fuck are you talkin bout?!" He continued to question as he ran from the belt. The water from the shower head splashed in his face causing him to gag.

"Ask Mya! That's where you bout to go ain't it? Well guess what! Find your own transportation! You ain't bout to be pullin up on bitches in my car! Wild ass nigga!"

Mya was another one of Marquee bootycalls, however, this time Parker found out. She was 18 going on 19 looking to be Marquee's number one. Mya resided in the suburbs deep in Clinton so Parker assumed that's how they met besides the minor chit chat they did on social media. Mya favored a bratz doll, her lips were plump and she had round bubble eyes just like Parker, however, Parker shit on her on her worst days. Mya stood about 5'0 exactly, her ass stuck out as did her boobs. The girl was fresh out of high school and worked at Wegmans. Parker wasn't one to judge be she was definitely stuck.

Parker ceased the beatings and walked out of the bathroom infuriated. Her blood was boiling and she just wanted Marquee out.

After she mentioned Mya he was on mute and had nothing to say.

February 26th, 2020

"Girl fuck him! Don't keep calling my phone with this bullshit if you going keep going back! Obviously it ain't goin get better girl! You gotta do what's best for you and Marquee ain't it!"

Parker laid across her bed with her feet kicked up as she sat on FaceTime with her good friend turned sister, Denim. If she couldn't count on nobody to keep it trill, she could always count on Denim. She was by the far the most brutally honest and straightforward person she knew. Plus, she'd been through her share of relationship dramas, so she was somewhat a little help.

It's had been 4 days since Parker put Marquee out. But that didn't last long, he apologized, moved his belongings back in and took her car in no time.

Parker knew her friend was right and she honestly didn't know her real reason for letting him back in. It definitely wasn't love but by far lust. Marquee had sex with a minor, not once but on several occasions according to the girl. To make matters worse he wore no condom and she's screaming she's with child now. Parker was beyond fed up but still she stayed.

DING!

DING!

DING!

DING!

Parker put Denim on hold and looked around the room in confusion. She knew Marquee had a new phone so the constant dings caught her off guard. It wasn't until she noticed his old phone lying under her bed.

"This bitch ass nigga lie so fuckin much yo! I could have sworn he said this shit was off!"

Parker unlocked the phone and to her surprise there were several unread text messages coming through from his text free app.

"Stupid ass nigga never logged out." Parker shook her head. Opening the text messages Parker' mouth dropped as she reread them over again.

"Hey Papi"

"How big is your chocolate?

PIC MAIL

PIC MAIL

"Wya I'm bout to come to you"

"I think I just might kill him." And there it was. Parker dropped her mouth and plopped onto her bed. She was lost for words. Not only was he sending pictures of his dick out, but to men at that.

It was official. He had crossed the line. Parker packed up his belongings and sat everything he owned on the sidewalk. She was done.

10pm that night

"Bitch I will kill you." Marquee threatened with clenched teeth. One hand wrapped around Parker's neck while he held his pistol to her head with the other hand. Parker stared down the barrel of his gun somewhat frightened for her life. *If he wanted me dead he would have pulled the trigger already, bitch ass nigga.*
They shot each other piercing stares both with resentment in their eyes. Releasing the grip from her neck Parker slid to the floor gasping for air. This was the last straw for her. What had once been a fairytale had turned into her worse nightmare. Months had gone by and Parker began to realize she didn't know the person she was lying next to every night. Marquee was scum, he was a horrible person, an amazing liar and master manipulator. Things were so good once upon a time. She wanted to be around him 24/7, they had so much fun. But Parker wanted more and she rushed things. She thought he was it and it had been her biggest learning experience.

P

The fact is, he won't let you go, but you need to stop letting
him stay.
He has no reason to let you go.
The reality is you provide some form of benefit to him and
he wants to keep it.
Whether it's a place to stay, money, stability, food, sex,
whatever the case may be.
He isn't going to be willing to give you what you need and
you're not demanding it because you allow him to do
nothing and still benefit.

Let's be real.
If he can't even give you half of what you give him why are
you continuously giving him what he desires?
Stop making it so easy for him.
Stop being so convenient for him.
Stop allowing him to make withdrawals without demanding
that he makes deposits back into you.
Mature relationships are all about reciprocity.
He will do what you allow him to.

Present Day, Therapy Session

"Okay, so let me get this straight." Ada twisted and turned in her seat. Parker rolled her eyes as she watched Lafonda make faces lowkey.

"This thing with the girl Reema." Ada paused and furrowed her eyebrows. "The same incident happened with Ivory?" She questioned.

"That's different." Parker replied.

"How so?" Ada didn't see the difference.

Parker sat up in her seat and began to explain. "Marquee and I were in an actual relationship. Him and Reema weren't."

"What's your point?" Ada sat with a straight and crossed arms. She continued to raise her eyebrows throughout the session as if she was confused.

"It's just different." Parker had no explanation she just knew the situation was set up different in her head.

Ada tucked her kinky twist behind her ears. "Let's be real Parker, this was your Karma. You loose em how you got em."

"Nah, that shit wit Ivory was deeper." Parker shook her head, her blood began to boil. Things still weren't sitting well with her. "That bitch conspired to kill me."

"I understand your anger and frustration." Ada attempted to empathize with Parker but was instantly shit down.

"Bitch please. You have no idea." Parker responded in a nasty tone.

"I do. You're hurt." She responded. "So, let's talk about it. Tell me about Ivory. How did that happen?"

JOURNAL ENTRY #3

What do you call a "friend" that fucks all their friends boyfriends behind their back?

Ines
Trifling
Sleezy hoe
Typical hoe
Disloyal
Fake whore
Scandalous
Wild bitch
Crummy bitch
Secret hater

That's not your friend, she's nobodies' friend. She doesn't even like herself to begin with. She wants to be everybody else.

Let me tell y'all why I don't fuck hoes. I don't fuck with hoes because they so sneaky and conniving. They'll sit in your face and fake fuck witchu, whole time they'll be feeling a way behind closed doors. These bitches will envy you and want everything you got, all while smiling in your face.

Two things you don't tell these bitches, you're next purchase, and the nigga you fuckin cus you can't trust these hoes for shit.

I love that lowkey shit, cause bitches love throwing pussy when they know who you fuck with. Keep my nigga in private, bitches scare me, they want to fuck on your nigga just cause he your nigga.

41

I like my nigga untouchable, do not be accessible to these low-life bitches. You become "That nigga" when bitches can't even get near you.

Buttttttt, when you're a bad bitch you'll intimidate a nigga and make him realize you're out of his league and now he's insecure so he's gonna fuck wit basic bitches to boost his ego and make him feel like that nigga.

I be stuck on shit cause it be the principle, like why did you even think the shit was cool and I'm a sucker for deep talks. I wanna know what made you think I was the bitch you were about to play with?

July 2020

Months had went by and Parker was still on his mind so he couldn't help but to be spiteful to get her attention. She knew the real him and some of his deepest darkest secrets and he wasn't letting her off the hook so easy. Little did he know she was just as determined to see him miserable.

In efforts to make her jealous Marquee decided to hook up with Ivory, Parker's last tech and well known associate. She was our typical dirty Mexican. Ivory was young wild and reckless she had no regards for anyone and she was nobodies friend. The little bitch was all for self and as trifling as they come. Parker was nothing but good to her, always a phone call away when she needed something and this is what she did in return. Ivory knew all about Marquee, specifically because Parker confided in her and that's where she fucked up.

Marquee parked his new navy blue 2013 BMV in the lot and made his way to Ivory unit. Upon entering he immediately grabbed her face and stuck his tongue inside her mouth. He was rough and loved nasty shit, as was Ivory. They made the perfect couple, two piss poor clowns.

Marquee had no idea just how dirty Ivory was. Her home looked as if it had been ransacked. Clothes were thrown around everywhere and there was a putrid smell coming from the master bedroom. She ate in her bed and couldn't pinpoint the last time she had changed her sheets. Not to mention, she hadn't seen the bottom of her sink in a very long time. It was safe to say that he was disgusted but under the circumstances and the living conditions at his mother's house, he was willing to settle.

After making himself comfortable and getting settled in he laid back on the messy sofa and Ivory attempted to bring Parker's name up.

"You talked to that bitch P?"

He smirked "naw, fuck her. But let me ask you something.

"What?"

"What Parker do to you? I thought y'all was friends, so why you here wit me?" He questioned. Parker was a genuine soul and often gullible so he could see how she would let it slide but he knew Ivory was a shiesty bitch.

"Quee please. We was cool we was cordial or watever. But don't none of that matter now, do it. Iont even know why you was fuckin wit her."

She silenced Marquee as she straddled him and removed her clothing. Lights out.

December 2020

Parker stopped passed Enterprise and picked up a Rental for a few hours. She had a night in store for her.

Gangsta Fever by NBA YoungBoy blared through her speakers and she lit her blunt. It was a must she eased her mind before these series of events took place. Arriving at the Heather Hills Apartment Complex, Parker pulled her rental directly next to Ivory car and patiently waited for her to come out.

About an hour after she strolled out, dressed to impress. It was 9:30 on the dot. Ivory flipped her hair and popped her gum. Her lip gloss shinned when the moonlight hit. Parker mugged her in disgust.

Parker and Ivory met through her longtime friend Rashad from high school, she happened to be his girlfriend at the time. Plus, they had a mutual friend as well, Bossy. Ivory was pretty as fuck with poor hygiene and low standards to top it off she was a whore. Still an adolescent she allowed Marquee to exploit her, and she also lost a friend along the way.

As she made it to her car, unlocking her door, she dipped inside paying no attention to her surroundings. Parker eased out of the vehicle and crept up on Ivory. Grabbing her forcefully from behind she quickly injected vicerony into her neck, her body instantly went limp.

Parker put the rental in cruise as she collected her thoughts. She had no idea how this would play out. Her emotions had gotten the best of her and she feared for the consequences. *"I just need to do this shit right and I'm straight."* She coached herself tightly gripping the steering wheel. Focusing on the road and keeping an eye out for anything unusual Parker made it to Rock Creek Park in no time. She parked her car alongside the trail. Wanting a few minutes to herself she got out and stood over the bridge. Rock creek was a tributary of the Potomac River. It emptied into the Atlantic Ocean via the Chesapeake Bay. The creek itself was magical in Parker's eyes. She enjoyed the scenery in each season.

Parker stuck her hands in her pockets as she shivered. *"How did I get here?"* She questioned herself. Pushing everything to the back of her mind she diverted all her focus to her main goal. She trugged back to the car and popped the trunk. Ivory lie there like a rag doll. Parker had bound her hands and feet together and stuck gorilla tape across her mouth. First, she grabbed the weight and dragged it to the edge of the bridge. She then went back for Ivory.

"What the hell did he see in you? Why you? Vicious ass bitch! Smiling in my face and fuckin my man behind my back. Well now y'all can have each other."

Without hesitation Parker yanked Ivory drugged body out of the trunk and dropped her to the ground. She picked up her feet and pulled her directly to the edge and tied a pretty knot around her ankles connecting the 50lb weight. Parker straddled her and smacked her face several times until she came to.

"Wakey wakey." Parker grinned sinisterly.

Ivory observed her surroundings and her eyes instantly widened. She was frightened for her life and Parker loved every minute of it.

She began to panic trying to release herself from the restraints.

"I feel bad for your son. Because now he'll grow up without a mommy." Parker taunted.

Parker watched the tears escape Ivory eyes but she didn't feel the slightest bit of sorry for the girl. "I told you I was going to get my lick back bitch." She rose to her feet and nudged Ivory one good time with her foot. There was a sudden loud thud. And just like that, she was gone. There was a weight lifted from her shoulders, Parker was relieved.

<u>Therapy Session</u>

Parker started blanky into space as she told Ada her story. With watery eyes, she struggled. "You never really know a person. Who would have known, like really? I've never in my life ever dealt with a male like Marquee and I don't mean that in a good way. This was nothing but an eye opener and a learning experience. If I could go back in time, I'd never even look his way. That was by far the most toxic relationship ever and I'm so glad I found my way out."

CHAPTER 2

ENDEARMENT

"Dreux"

JOURNAL ENTRY #4

It hurts. A lot !! And you can't do anything about it.
Everyone who has had a lover or a crush can relate to this. The pain just sits there and you can't do anything about it. A mere thought of him/her is enough to send you spiraling into depression.

Therapy Session

"What was your happiest relationship?" Ada asked trying to dig a little deeper into her past.

"Dreux, most definitely." Parker began to reminisce. Her eyes watered as she thought about him. "We were so happy under the conditions and circumstances."

"And then?"

"And then he left me." Parker confessed.

"How did that make you feel?" Ada questioned.

"Hurt, abandoned mainly, depressed very depressed. I loved him so much"

"Why'd he leave?"

"He was doin what was best for him."

"How so?"

Ada did her best to pry and get to the bottom of Parker's troubles. However, after a few hours, she was finally warming up and letting her in.

January 30th, 2017

Parker slowly inhaled and exhaled the smoke as she passed the blunt to Shawn. They had met at IHOP during training for the 1st time and instantly clicked. Shawn was 5 years her senior and was just as hood as she could be. Her dreads fell down her back and she had decal holes in her face from surface piercings. Her lips were permanently purple from all the weed and cigarettes she smoked constantly due to stress and she was kind of heavy set in some areas.

They had hot boxed Parkers Coupe after work while sitting on the Main Street of Ridge Rd. Shawn was about to introduce Parker to her best friend DD. From 6th St. Often they crashed at her Aunt Winne house around 37th. Aunt Winne was the carefree aunt that let you do damn near whatever the hell you wanted. She lived in a 1bedroom apartment with her sister Lina and her longtime on and off boyfriend Miguel. Lina was the youngest of the siblings while Winne was the middle child, leaving Ro, DD's mom the oldest.

Winne was the alcoholic out of the bunch. She had some type of liquor in her cup every day of the week all throughout the day and slept with different dudes around the way. Lina did the same, except only when she wasn't in a committed relationship with Miguel. He had many insecurities due to pass traumas with his mother which caused a strain on their relationship constantly. Miguel was from Gault Pl., he was your normal hang banger, but he wasn't smart with his money at all ever, it was always spent on frivolous materials leaving him broke. DD was the heavy set cousin that was known for beating people into shape. She resembled one of the grudge sisters from the proud family movie; not a pretty sight to see.

Despite growing up in the city as a younger child, Parker was still a Maryland girl, but she couldn't get enough of the city. It gave her a rush, it made her feel free.

Immediately after their session Shawn gathered her belongings and exited the car as did Parker. The stench of hot sour piss filled her nostrils. They stepped over garbage scattered on the sidewalk as she followed behind Shawn.

The normal junkies stood in front of their buildings and paced up and down the steps while they were on the way into Winnie's building. It was Parker's first time on this side of Minnesota Ave, if was all foreign to her.

"Nigga get the fuck out my house Dwayne! I told you I don't want you doin that shit in my house!" Tootsie shouted while spit flew from her mouth. She had two teeth left that were apparently hangin on for dear life. Tootsie gave birth to 15 children and was shaped like a pair of scissors.

Before they could step foot inside the building, they were met by Tootsie in the entrance throwing Wayne's belongings outside.

He had fucked up one too many times smoking that shit. PCP was one hell of a drug and tootsie wasn't having it on her watch.

Shawn grabbed Parker's hand and yanked her through the door. She knocked twice and the door opened. Before they could get completely in smoke filled Parker's nostrils and she squinted her eyes. Several people filled the tiny apartment.

"Wasssup Bitch!" DD stood at 6 feet exactly, the girl was huge. She threw her arms up and waddled over to Shawn grinning. They embraced each other. Parker stood in the corner behind Shawn and made herself familiar with her surroundings. Everyone had been so engaged in their own conversations, they paid Parker no mind. It wasn't until she diverted her focus elsewhere, something caught her eye.

"That's right boy! That what the fuck I'm talkin bout!" Pito cheered himself on as he was winning a game he had bets on earlier in the day.

"Aye Ma, lemme get a beer yo!" He shouted in Winnie's direction and she did as she was told.

At first it was just his voice that was so intriguing to her, it was his up north accent. But when he turned his back and they locked eyes Parker was in a daze. *"Holy shit, is this real?"* Pito's vanilla toned body was covered in graffiti. From his arms, to his chest and his neck. Puerto Rican and African American born, his hair waved up and laid perfectly on his head. His eyes were beady and he had a nose like Omar Wilson, but it wasn't that bad.

"Damn, who is that?"

Pito was originally from CT. That's where his entire family was from. It was still a mystery how his mother and aunts traveled to the city. With no stability and the recent loss of his grandmother, Pito became a product of his environment and hopped in the streets. He had a thing for weed but made majority of his money from cocoaine. But here he was, for how long wasn't a question Parker had been worried about at the time, although she should have.

December 2017
Parker gathered her belongings and exited her car. She had been working the mid-day shifts at her job because she couldn't seem to get up early in the morning. Working as a concierge definitely had its pros and cons but it was doable for the time being. Parker descended the steps and made her way to Winnies building, before she made it to the last step she overheard Tootsie cussing Wayne out; he was getting high again. Parker couldn't get enough, she had a love/hate relationship with the city but this is where she got most of her entertainment.

It had almost been a year since Parker and Dreux started dealing with each other and she was so happy. Their relationship was healthy and the communication was on point, for the most part they had become the best of friends. When they were away from one another it felt awkward so Pito asked her to stay. Since then Parker only went home every once in a blue moon.

It was a lituation everyday around 37th but today it had been rather quiet. Parker used a key Winne gave her months prior to let herself in. Once Parker entered the room fell silent and all eyes were on her. Pito sat across from an older man that looked identical to him.

"This Parker. This my girl." Pito rose from his seat and stood next to Parker.

The man smiled and nodded his head.

"Parker," Pito paused. "This my dad."

Parker's eyes widened, and she was lost for words.

"Oh shit"

Parker had heard all the stories from each family member. Macho was the grim reaper. He had his hands in everything you could think of from drugs and real estate to people. His looks were in fact very much deceiving. He resembled El Chapo in stature; short man and he aged well so he didn't look half as close to 50. Macho wasn't flashy, he didn't like to draw attention. He wore navy blue khakis with a white tee and 990s; pretty regular. When you looked at him the last thing you would suspect is that he's a millionaire; that's exactly what he wanted you to think.

"Nice to meet you Parker." He extended his hand and Parker returned the gesture.

**

Cooped up in the one bedroom, Parker stretched across the full-size mattress next to Lina. Pito and Macho had been discussing something Parker felt was rather important.

"I can't believe he here." Winne grinned while throwing her drunk back.

Lina turned up her nose. "Bitch he ain't here for you."

Winne and Macho had a difficult love story. Back then she was his ride or die, they were Bonnie and Clyde. But Macho had to go back to Puerto Rico and he left Winne with a baby. Distraught, she turned to alcohol. Macho eventually returned for the sake of his son, but he wanted nothing to do with Winne. If pained him to see what she had made of herself and how the alcohol ruined her.

"I know but.." Winne threw her head against the wall. Before she could finish her sentence lay cut her off. "Nuts, shut up." Lina hit the volume on the tv and we all diverted our focus to love and hip hop.

**

Pito eased in bed next to Parker and hugged her from behind. The meeting with his father had left him not only ecstatic but sad as well. Just as Parker, he too had gotten attached.

He squeezed her tight and gently placed kisses all over her. He watched her sleep, she snored lightly. Pushing the hair from out her face caused her to jump out of her sleep.

"Why the hell are you up?" Parker questioned him with one eye open and the other closed.

He dropped his head, Parker could sense it was something bothering him. She rolled over to face him but still kept her eyes shut.

"Talk to me babe.."

"I'm leaving." Parker shot up in confusion.

"Leaving and going where?" She questioned.

"East coast"

And just like that. Her was here one min and gone the next. Macho had offered him the proposition of a lifetime and he accepted it. He would choose anything over sleeping on his mama couch around 37th in a one bedroom apartment with his girlfriend. He didn't leave because he didn't want to be with Parker. If he could take her, he sure would have but he knew that wasn't an option.

"I love you P and I promise I'm coming back for you. Just give me some time to get everything in order." He assured.

January 2018

Time had flown by and Parker dreaded pitons last days in dc.

They lie in bed that night, Pito squeezed her tight as she draped one leg across his. The room was pitch black and silence filled the room. Parker allowed her tears to freely flow. She was a hurting inside and had no idea how to control it. Pito ran his fingers through her hair and gently kissed her forehead. He continued to hold her and console her.

Parker's thoughts ran wild as she tried to figure out her next move. He had been doing what was best for him now it was her turn.

**

The ride to BWI was draining. They rode in silence and there was heavy traffic due to rush hour.

Pito looked Parker in her eyes before he snatched her into his arms. He squeezed her and they rocked back and forth. It was early January, the temperature was below feeezing but Parker didn't mind.

"I guess this is goodbye." She managed to get out. Parked sobbed and tears stained her face.

Pito sighed "Naw baby this ain't goodbye Parker I promise." Pito was just as frustrated with his situation but he had no choice.

"I love you so much Parker. You the best thing that ever happened to me." He stood there and let her cry for a few more mins.

"Baby I gotta go."

March 2018

Parker sulked in her misery for 2 months straight Distraught and depressed. She isolated herself and avoided those closest to her.

She barely showed her faces around 37th anymore, it all reminded her of him and she hated it. Although they were still together Parker knew eventually things wouldn't last. She also knew he wouldn't be coming back. Their calls became shorter and texts became dry. He was on the West Coast living his best vigilante lifestyle, meanwhile Parker was stuck back in the DMV.

December 25th, 2020

"Merry Christmas Parker. I miss you and I love you. I know I left and was supposed to come back, and I never did. For that I am sorry. Shit been fucked up for me my entire life. When I saw the opportunity for a better life, I took it and ran with it. It may not seem like it, but it hurts being away from you girl. If I had the option to bring you with me I would have, no questions. I love you girl. We love you, you apart of the family now. We locked in forever Parker, I love you for life and I'm honored that I got to experience my first real relationship with an amazing individual. But I ain't goin hold you up, I'm proud of you babes and all of your accomplishments. Don't stop. I love you and I'll see you soon. Merry Christmas P"

CHAPTER 3

FORTUITOUS

"Jaahar"

P

I deserved every L I took.
I got too comfortable with things I shouldn't have.

Therapy Session

"Jaahar ass was unexpected. He popped up right after Dreux left for Cali." Parker laughed.

"Why is this one funny?" Ada asked confused.

"Because that man was something else, really a different breed." she continued to giggle dramatically.

"What do you mean?"

"I mean..." Parker paused to roll her eyes. "I never dealt wit a nigga like him before. So raw, straightforward and unbothered...literally. He was the most honest person ever I had no choice but to respect it and that's why I fucked wit him. He always kept it 100 and never sugar coated shit wit me.

I was just a dummy ya know, I caught feelings. I knew there would never be a relationship and I didn't want one tuhhhh not wit his ass." she explained.

"The Lil bitch Bianca introduced me to him."

Lafonda rose her eyebrow. "This is the same Bianca that you and Ivory were mutual friends with?"

Parker shook her head. "Correct."

April 2018

Parker pulled into the Fort Chaplin complex parking lot. She Parked nearest to the door as always, she dreaded the long walks. Bianca had invited her over to join in on a double date. It had been months since Dreux had moved to the West Coast, she figured she'd have to get out her funk sooner or later so she took her up on the offer.

Bianca was a wild one and always full of surprises, so she had no idea what to expect. Parker and Bianca had only known each other for a short period of time but clicked instantly. But Parker noticed a change after the father of her kids had passed away. She found comfort in a new guy and he just happened to beat females. Ever since she's been living her life on the edge.

After letting herself in Bianca met her halfway.

"What's goin on miss girl?" She greeted Parker in good spirits. Passing the kitchen she noticed dinner on the stove. She could smell turkey wings and baked macaroni. Hakim was seated at the dining room table rolling up. Bianca guided Parker to the entertainment area and there he was, New Jersey's Finest.

"Damn wassup witchu mamas" Jaahar licked his lips and scooted closer to Parker on the sofa.

She liked them dark, but his pale skin and demeanor turned her on. He exuded so much confidence and he was straightforward. His hair fell down his back, his chink eyes were hazel, and his plump lips were alluring and dimples deep.

Jaahar was from Camden New Jersey. He was a crip and a dedicated Muslim. To put the icing on the cake he was a street nigga who had his hands in almost everything you could think of. Jaahar had family all up and down on the East Coast. Recently his mother purchased some property in VA and that's how he met Hakim.

"Wassup" Parker responded hesitantly. From there it was a wrap.

They exchanged numbers and kept in contact. Bianca's idea was to get Parker's mind off of Dreux. She didn't figure Parker would go as far as trying to take things seriously but that's the kind of girl she was; a relationship girl.

July 2018

After a few minutes of fellating him, by which this time his manhood was standing straight up in attention, Parker withdrew, and let Jaahr take charge again. He laid Parker down, and spreading her legs, he got in between them. Then holding his cock in his hands, he touched her entrance, and slowly glided it inside. Without warning he began drilling Parker with his weapon. Because of the severe teasing that she had got before, it didn't take too long for her to orgasm, and he pulled out once she did, still hard. Next, he made her climb up on the couch with her hands on the back-rest, as he kneeled back. Then he positioned himself behind Parker, as he guided himself inside her again, this time from behind. Soon he was pounding her again, holding her hips and pulling her back every time he thrust in, and it took few minutes before Parker came once again, this time in near unison.

By the time they were done, it was past midnight.

**

"I told you what it was from the jump P. I fuck witchu, straight up. But as far as being the only female in my life, that ain't goin happen." He spoke with confidence and stood firm on his answer. "That's just me that's just who I am. On top of that it's my religion."

Parker rolled her eyes. "Nigga don't know where in the Quran do it say *"I can have any bitch I want as long as I take of them all."* You said that."

Jaahar laughed and blushed, his deep dimples and pearly white teeth did something to Parker. He was so fuckin smooth and laid back she loved everything about it.

"You want to be the only woman in my life P? Is that what it is?" He giggled.

"Very much so, what you think nigga?" She snapped.

"Listen let me tell you something, we locked in. I fuck witchu for life relationship or not and I mean that shit." He said sternly.

September 2018

"Wassup Mamí I need you." Jaahar spoke loud thru the phone. Parker twisted and turned in bed. It was past midnight, her and tony weren't on the best of speaking terms so she had no idea why he had been calling her. "I'm at Strip club, my car got fucked up and I cashed out on the bitches." He confessed.

Jaahar was by far the most straightforward blunt person she had ever met. He never knew what to say out his mouth and that bothered Parker at times.

Parker sucked her teeth "we'll ask one of the bitches you cashed out on for help!" She snapped back.

"Come on Mamí don't be like that, I need you Mamí." Jaahar begged and pleaded.

Parker shot up out of bed and was on her way. She loved the fact that he had practically begged her, she felt needed.

Strip clubs are the epitome of an adult playground. Parker pulled into the parking lot and found a spot. A mixture of visitors, strippers, bartenders, and junkies filled the parking lot. Before Parker could pick up her phone to tell Jaahar she had arrived, Out the corner of her eye she caught him hugged up with Norma jeans very own.

In the DMV there were a huge mix of girls who danced. Majority are college students, and many are single moms paying bills, the other half are simply lost souls being pimped out. Sad, but true.

Infuriated Parker exited the car and stormed over to the side of the building where the random girl had tony pinned against the wall.

"Excuse me!" Parker shouted causing the girl to jump and back away from tony. He laughed and his face lit up when he saw Parker.

"Mamí come join us." Parker stopped in her tracks and looked at Jaahar in amazement. He reached for her hand and she snatched it away.

He shook his head and dismissed the random. "I'll holla at you shorty." She batted her lashes and but her lip, right before she gave Parker the middle finger.

Jaahar wrapped his arm around Parker's shoulder and used her to keep himself up. He smelt horrible; the stench of tequila hit her nose hard and he wrecked of pussy and underarms. Disgusted, she threw him off of her.

"Son where the fuck is your car?" Parker was irritated and ready to be back in her bed at this point.

Jaahar slurred and couldn't walk in a straight line. "It's at the room."

Parker ran her fingers threw her hair "What room Jaahar?"

"I took one of the lil stripper jawns back to the room and my car fucked up. I told you." He explained.

Parker was lost for words. "You what? Don't even answer that."

She left him standing where he was, jogged to her car and pulled off.

What all strippers have in conmen as a group is that you can pretty much take 85-95% back to your hotel if you know how to play it, time it right and are willing to pay. They're drinking and are happy to leave the club at some point if you have game and Jaahar had it all. Cash, class, clean cut and an overall sweetheart.

Parker rode down 50 in awe making her way back home. *"I really can't believe this shit."* At a strip club, everything is for sale, even if the girls themselves don't always know it.

P

Do not settle,
Know and embrace your worth.
Do not entertain any man's nonsense.

P

You never know what God is saving you from.

CHAPTER 4

<u>SIDE BITCH CHRONICLES</u>

"Tahj"

ℙ

SIDE BITCH (English)
Noun (plural. Side Bitches)

1. A woman that is one level above a jump off but always a step below the wifey; girlfriend
A side bitch must know her part. She does not get holidays, birthdays. Etc. While he may meet your family, You will never meet his. A side bitch is a woman who will have sex Feb 1st through the 13th and spend Valentine's day alone.

2. When a girl is not exactly his girl.
Someone he treats as he should his girl bit never commits to her
She usually feels like shit

3. A female who is having a romantic or sexual relationship with another females significant other or spouse. She may truly be in love with the "taken" individual. The "taken" person may or may not reciprocate the feelings, but remains nonetheless that he has a "main girl" and is cheating on her with this female.

4. Side bitch is a female who can't get a man of her own so she settles on being a fuck

JOURNAL ENTRY #5

Are y'all ready for my first ghetto lesson?

*First things first, males use "Main Bitch" and "side bitch"
interchangeably.*

But that's only depending on how many "bitches" he actually has.

But I'm sure we all can agree that there are several clear differences.

*What's the first thing that comes to your mind when you think of a
"side bitch" or a "mistress"?*

Worst feeling in the world.

*So, a nigga can have a wife right; she gets majority of his time, affection,
money, she's the mother of his children, all that good stuff. She would
presumably be his "main bitch".*

*Then there's the "side bitch"; she only gets some of his time, a little
affection or probably just his money.*

But let's not forget about the third bitch or the rest of his "bitches".

*He may be only seeing them for sexual purposes, or he thinks he's so
lowkey to the point where he feels like he can juggle several different
bitches at once.*

*As a female, when you start fucking with a dude it comes to the point
where your together 24/7, you're having sex with this person and your
waking up to them, you're doing things that couples do, and you start
catching feelings.*

But, however, there is no title.

*When thinking of a side chick, mistress, or jump-off, the first thing
thought that comes to mind Is usually, homewrecker, slut, whore, or
some other derogatory term to describe this immoral woman who uses her
feminine wiles to attract and monopolize the attention of a married man
or an otherwise involved man.*

That's the easiest way to justify the actions of these women.

To understand the sidechick, one must first understand what makes a man want to have a woman on the side in the first place. You see, there can be no jump-off or mistress, without a man that is open to having one. It is your job as a woman who only desires to be the "ONLY chick," to not get involved with a man who is capable of having a side chick.

Therapy Session

Parker threw her head back and let it rest. She sighed loud and deeply as she shut her eyes. "Dealing with Tahj was nothing but an experience. From his family, to his kids, to his baby mommas; that shit was a mess okay." she paused. "Now I thought Dreux's family was somewhat dysfunctional but they ain't got shit on the Johnson's. In the beginning shit was all peaches and cream wit his ass and towards the end that shit became intolerable. It was amazing, literally a rush, that was until I found myself on the run and his ultimate side bitch."

"On the run?" Ada screeched in confusion.

"I let that shit happen. I ain't even mad. That was nothing but a learning experience."

April 2019

"Girl come the fuck on! It's getting late!" Parker rushed her cousin Brooke. They had worked the night shift at their part time job; a shabby rundown bar on Benning Rd. She went to school, got her license and instantly hit the bartending scene. She enjoyed it for the most part, and it kept her busy . Besides, Dreux had been gone for a while and Parker was starting to get back to herself. She was single and just wanted to have some fun.

It was 1am on the dot and they were headed to the strip in Baltimore. The hottest strip clubs and food spots sat on this wing. Parker had only been to Baltimore a few times but never in the city. It was by far dirtier than the DC. Junkies and garbage covered the streets. The smell was atrocious. The streets were bumpy and the roads were narrow. However, the nightlife was something else. It may not have been Las Vegas but it had some of the topnotch strip clubs.

They made their way inside The Penthouse, Baltimore's #1 gentlemen's club. It featured the most beautiful women, they offered private dances, a full bar, diverse champagne lists, VIP rooms, executive suites, full nude cabaret and more. Brooke grabbed Parker's hand and let her to the dimly lit back where the actual club was. There was a marble-and-mirror stage which featured topless and bikini dancers, there was a curtained off private lap dancers areas. In addition, there were rooms where dancers would perform full service nude private "peep shows" for customers, separated by one-way glass mirrors.

A good forty-five minutes had gone by and they were seven shots it. Future had been thumping through the speakers and Parker was feeling exactly right; she was enjoying herself. Out the corner of her eye she focused her attention on what seemed to be like the man of the hour. Bystanders moved and cleared the walkway for the entourage, they moved with such confidence. Parker happened to lock eyes with the man in charge, he caught her eye as well. Him and his crew headed upstairs, but he didn't let Parker out of his sight. For the rest of the night, she indulged in more shots with Brooke until they were almost too intoxicated to make it home. Right before Parker could hand the bartender her card and unfamiliar voice whispered in her ear and grabbed her hand. "I got it.." Tahj whispered.
He sent shivers up Parker's spine. Tahj pulled out 3 $100 bill and handed it to the bartender. Brooke raised her eyebrows and made faces. "Oh okay I know that's right."
Parker shook her head and laughed as she extended her hand. "Parker." She slurred.

"Tahj." He grabbed her hand and rubbed it. "Look I gotta go but give me your number, I'm tryin' take you out."

Parker didn't hesitate not one bit all though she should have. "*BINGO! He's the big dawg and I want him*" Parker said to herself. But little did she know, she was in for a rude awakening.

<u>May 18th, 2019</u>

Tahj was consistent for the most part. He even hit Parker up the same night to make sure she made it in safe. They texted throughout the day and got to know each other somewhat.

Parker received a weird call from Tahj, he had been demanding to see her and that the matters were urgent. Parker figured he wanted some pussy and she was going to milk his ass for everything he had.

She pulled into Franklin Park, the boujie hood apartment complex in Greenbelt Md. They had two-star reviews on the net, mice, roaches and bad management. Parker knew because she had a friend that occupied a unit.

She pulled into a spot in front of the building he gave her and waited for him to come out. Momentarily he eased out of the door and swayed to her car. He sported a Nike tech sweatsuit and paired it with some Nike AirMax. His arms were covered in tattoos, she could tell he needed a hair cut by the way it had grown out; it was very much Italian hair.

He got in the car and his face lit up. Parker took in his features; she knew she had to have been fucked up because she totally forgot what he had looked like. Although he was fine, he just wasn't her type at all. Parker like them dark as fuck, Tahj, was as pale as he could be. He teeth threw her off for the most part, they were almost perfect with the exception of his midget tooth. But she couldn't get enough of his freckles, they set the tone.

"Wassup witchu Miss Parker?" He had a strong Baltimore accent and she hated it in the worst way. She laughed on sight and couldn't catch her breath. "Awww your accent."

he shook his head. "I knew you would say that."

She got herself together, "so wassup, what's goin on?"

"Mannnn..." he took a long loud sigh, "shit a mess."

Parker sat there and stared blankly at him. "Okay, you goin elaborate."

He looked Parker in her eyes, for the second time ever they locked eyes. "I need to know if I can trust you." He replied. Seconds went by and he broke the silence. He popped up from the seat and began to exit the car.

"Come on." He waved for her to get out the car.

Parker sat there for a minute before she moved. "Huh" she continued to sit in confusion. "Where are we going?"

"Just come on!" He demanded and Parker did as she was told. She grabbed her purse and followed behind Tahj into the building. She looked behind her once more and locked her doors.

"You bout to meet my step mother and shit." He stated dryly.

He slowed his steps and cautiously entered as if he didn't want her to know anyone was there. Parker was right on his heels. The blinds were open so the light from outside allowed you to see the living room, which had been completely empty. It had only been occupied by three book bags and a full-size air mattress that was very much deflated. Before she could finish observing the empty house the lights flickered on and the sight before her made Parker jump. She had no idea what she walked into.

"Awwwww hiiiii you so pretty." Neecy sauntered over to Parker with a beer in one hand and a cigarette in the other. She too had a strong Baltimore accent. Her hairline had been receding and she colored it turquoise. He eyes were gigantic as if they could have been falling out of the sockets. And she had large moles plastered on her face. Neecy was fairly darkskin, her feet were bout as ashy as Mr. Browns kneecaps, and she had no care in the world.

Parker didn't know how to react or what to say to respond so she just stood there and cracked a smile.

"So, what's your name sweet?" Neecy took a puff of her cigarette and blew the smoke in Parker's face.

"Parker" she coughed in response.

"Ohhhh oakyyyyy that's cute." She batted her eyelashes at Parker and continued to smoke the cigarette. She picked in her hair and twirled around in her dingy robe. It was beady as hell and looked about one hundred years old.

Diverting her attention back to Parker.

"So I don't usually allow people in my house but my step son said you good." She got close to Parker and smile showing her rotten teeth. The way the plaque had built up around her gums was horrible. Parker's stomach turned and she held her breath so she for sure wouldn't get a width of anything. She slightly backed up and shook her head in agreeance to whatever point she had been trying to get at.

Tahj had been distracted by the constant phone calls he was receiving. Parker took a seat on the air mattress and watched Moe glide back into her bedroom.

"Uh hello?" Parker waved her hands in the air trying to get his attention.

"My bad, that was my baby mom." He said dryly turning to face toward Parker.

Her mouth dropped in confusion. *"Kids? Is he serious? I wonder how many what the hell!"*
"So how many kids do you have?" She asked curiously.
"two, 5 and 1."
"Oh damn," her eyes widened. Parker had never experienced baby momma drama before but she didn't want there to be a first time.

**

Parker had caught sight of Tahj's bulge in his pants, and the thought of what could happen if she loosened her morals was too tempting. He got her jeans off, and then took her own clothes off, leaving both of them in inner-wear. Then he began teasing Parker over my panties, tracing their outline, dragging his fingers over them but just not over her lower lips. In time, he unhooked her bra, and squeezed her breasts gently in his hands, as he began licking her bare nipples, till they stiffened and became rock-hard. By now, Parker was soaking wet, and she was glad he considered that she was still over-dressed, and decided to slide off her panties. Then he spread her legs wide, pinning them with his hands, as he positioned himself between Parker and began a series of long licks over her inner thighs. And then finally it began happening — Parker began to feel the warmness of his long, raspy tongue lapping at her labia after several months of celibacy. Every lick sent electric sparks up her belly and they exploded into her brain, as he kept licking at it, taking Parker closer and closer but never making her cum, getting her increasingly desperate while his tongue licked on her lips and clit, while Parker was purring in ecstasy.

**

It was 3Am on the dot, Parker rolled over and noticed the side of the air mattress Tahj had been sleeping on was empty, so she shot him a text. Unable to keep her eyes open she knew he couldn't have gone far so she drifted back off into a deep sleep.

Not too far into her nap she was awakened by the authorities. "POLICE! We have a search warrant!" Officer 1 shouted. Without any further warning 12 came bursting thru the doors.

"Get down! Get down on the ground now!" They shouted. It seemed like everything had been moving in slow motion. They swarmed the place in a matter of seconds. Parker jumped up revealing her half naked body but the quickly tackled her to the ground. Miss Neecy was face down handcuffed while an officer had his foot resting on her head. Parker was stuck, she was lost for words, she had no moves. Tahj built a drug empire in Baltimore that generated more than 4 million in profits. He was in bed with the Chinese, money launderers and the Mexican drug cartel pushing cocaine, heroin and fentanyl in the city and surrounding counties. He was the big dog, he was ringleader, he called the shots. He brought 25 to 50 kilos of drugs into Baltimore every month. And for that very reason, they were out to get him.

**

Parker sprinted to her car and jumped in the passenger seat. Before she could close the door Tahj sped off causing her head to jerk back something serious.

"Tahj what the fuck!" Parker shouted! "Explain yourself!"

"Ain't nothing to explain Parker! I'm on the run!" He fired back.

"On the run?" She paused "nigga is you serious!"

"I told you I had some shit goin on!" Tahj looked exhausted and frustrated. He didn't know what his next move was going to be or where he would go but it wasn't Baltimore.

77

He was fucked up, the feds blitzed his spot and took his last little piece of change.

They rode for 45 mins and stopped at a hotel in the city. Parker wasn't turning down the offer, so she straightened her attitude up and went with the flow. Once they were checked in, they headed up to their suite and both showered.

Distinctive marks on Tahj's neck instantly caught her attention.

"What the fuck is that on your neck?" She questioned.

Tahj stood in bathroom with a blank expression, he was lost for words.

Parker stood there with the same expression waiting for an answer. "Uh hello? Are you dumb or deaf?"

Tahj sighed and dropped his head in frustrations. "My babymova did it." He confessed. "But it ain't even like that." He lied.

Parker stood there in amazement. "So that's where you was at last night?" She paused. "While I was at your stepmothers house on the floor on an air mattress, you were with the mother of your children, oh let's not forget SWAT kicked down doors and tussled us to the ground looking for your ass." Parker spat! She was beyond through. She couldn't believe she was in this predicament.

"Nah my youngest son mom did this to my neck. I went to grab the weed and see my son."

Parker's mouth dropped. "Hold on, you got two different baby moms?"

"Yea" he replied.

Parker turned her back and got in bed. She pondered on the past 8 hours and didn't know what to think.

"What a complete shit show! I knew he was gettin it but this is overrated." It was 7am on the dot and Parker had barely gotten any sleep so she felt now was the perfect time.

May 2018

The county differed from the city in many ways, it was mainly the boujie part of Baltimore. They drove down Balt-Wash Pkwy until they hit Ellicott City. Parker knew for sure they were in the suburbs from the distinct surroundings. The grass was greener, the air smelled fresh, and the people were friendly; although Parker didn't care too much for red necks. They were in route to his mother's house, from the last incident Parker had no idea what to expect.

"Get the fuck out my house! Ima have my son whoop yo ass! And that ain't my grandson!" Trina shouted. You could hear commotion and muffled screams outside. They were shouting to the top of their lungs. Tahj rushed to the door with Parker on his heels. Making a grand entrance he was face-to-face with the love of his life and babymomma from hell!

Tahj threw his head back and ran his hands through his hair. "Sienna I told you to drop my son off and leave."

"Mmm hmm I told her ass to get on! She the reason you in this bullshit now!" Trina chimed in to instigate.

Trina was nothing to play with, she was definitely not the one. At the age of 56, after giving birth to four children she was stacked. Parker noticed her waist shaper and figured she had gotten surgery not too long ago. Trina was a full-bred Italian and as sassy and quick-witted as they came. She too was small in stature but thick. She favored Sandra Bullock, it was mainly her facial features. Her eyes were beady like Tahj's, four teeth were missing on the right side of her mouth and her unibrow had started to show itself to the world.

She had it out for Sienna from day one, she never liked the girl. For one there was a major age difference and Trina didn't like the way Sienna carried herself.

"First of all!" Sienna snapped back "Ya momma keep screaming it Ean ain't ya son! I ain't goin have too much more of that shit!" She defended herself.

Sienna was short and shapely in all the right places. Her ass stuck out and her breast sat up. You could tell she was some sort of Asian decent. Her hair fell down her back and her eyes almost looked shut the way they were slanted. She had deep dimples and a chubby face. Bowlegged and standing at 4'ft, she was everything Sienna wanted and more to be honest. Age was nothing but a number for him.

The feud between the two ladies had been brewing for years now. Sienna despised Trina just as much as Trina despised her.

"Daddyyyyyy!" Louis shouted scurrying down the steps. He leaped in his arms and hugged him tight. Right behind him but a little slower was Ean. Both boys took after their mother, Tahj's genes were weak, his children looked nothing like him.

"Ahhhhh wassup boys! I miss y'all" Tahj scooped them both up and embraced them while showering them with kisses.

"Where have you been? I haven't seen you in so long!" Louis questioned.

The room fell silent. Tahj had no response; he didn't know how to tell Louis he wouldn't see him for a while. Sienna cracked a slight chuckle before she made her unnecessary comment. "On the run."

"Let's not forget you the reason!" Trina shot back. "If only you could have just kept your mouth shut you little twit!"

Trina was right, Sienna was the reason Tahj was hemmed up in the first place. She gave the feds the drop on Tahj by an

80

accident all because she couldn't keep her mouth shut. Now he was looking at life and she was the reason.

Louis stared at Parker for a few seconds before his curiosity took over. "Daddy who's that? he tapped Tahj shoulder and pointed in Parker's direction causing everyone to divert their focus on her.

"Yea who is that Tahj?" Sienna looked Parker up and down and mugged her. She crossed her arms and rolled her eyes while she waited for an explanation.

Tahj sucked his teeth "mind your business Sienna."

"You are my business!" She shouted "you move on fast! This must be the new bitch you been creeping around wit." Sienna investigated trying to get more information.

"Good! As long as he ain't wit you, bitch." Trina mumbled under her breath loud enough for everyone to hear.

"You know what" Sienna threw her purse over her shoulder and snatched Ean from Tahj's arms. "I'm taking my son and I'm leaving." She gathered his belongings.

Trina stood on the bottom step with an ice-cold brew in her hand with a lit cigarette. She shook her head. "You just goin let her take your son?" Trina taunted Tahj.

"Miss Trina you are crazy! Just a minute ago you ain't want my son here and he wasn't your grandson! Now you got a problem with me taking my child? Bitch, please save that shit" Sienna responded in her defense. She swung Ean across her hip and pranced to the door with bags in her hand. Tahj sat Louis down and scurried behind Sienna. He forcefully grabbed her arm and threw her against the wall with their son in her arms. Tahj grabbed her by the neck and looked her in the eyes. "You better not say shit in court either Sienna." He whispered but with meaning as he released the grip he had on her.

She straightened herself out and opened the door. Before she departed, she made eye context with Parker. "And bitch I ain't goin nowhere." She left her with those last words and Parker couldn't do anything but laugh.

"If this ain't the messy shit I've ever encountered."

**

Parker sat on the edge of the bed awkwardly while Kenny observed her. Kenny was Tahj older gay brother, they were two years apart and inseparable. As Kenny got older throughout the years he came out and his parents shunned him as an outcast.

He was tall about 6'2 and paler than ever. He modeled and did makeup, in fact he was one of the few professionals in the county. Kenny took after the father as far as his looks; his eyes were beady while his lips were thick and round, he kept himself shaved on a daily. His face resembled a baby's ass. It was safe to say he kept himself up.

"So, you're the side bitch?" Kenny sat with his legs crossed and a jay in his hand. "I've heard so much about you."

Parker was taken aback by his comment. "Excuse me?"

"Oh..." Kenny covered his mouth and batted his eyelashes. "I didn't mean that as an insult."

Parker sat there in confusion, she stared at him blankly and waited for the remainder of the response.

"Well? What did you mean?"

"Girl" Kenny waved her off and crossed his legs back. "My brother likes you." He pulled his cigarette. "But he also still in love with Sienna. Plus, he got a lot of shit wit him." Kenny was straightforward and honest. He had no cut cards for anyone.

Parker's eyes widened and she scrunched her eyebrows together.

Kenny shook his head up and down as he rocked back and forth in his old rocking chair.

"I love him to death, but that nigga got a lot of shit with him girl, I'd advise you to get out while you can." He coached. Her words had gotten caught in her throat. She had no response, nothing to say. She didn't know what to say actually.

**

"What a fuckin night" Parker thought to herself. She joined Tahj and his eldest son Louis in the living room on his mother's couch.

For the most part, the sides Parker had seen of Tahj were amazing. He was compassionate, affectionate, genuine, and he was a great father; however, he was still somewhat distant with Parker which made her think about the conversation with Kenny earlier. Three sudden knocks at the door caused Parker to jump out of her thoughts.

"Tisha get the door!" Tahj shouted.

Tisha was Tahj's older sister by five years. Although mentally challenged, she was the prettiest thing. "Ooo-oo-k Taa-ah-j" She stuttered walking to the door with her hands propped up in front of her chest.

She looked through the peep hole and gasped loudly in excitement. She clapped her hands and before she could turn the knob Jesscia came bursting through the door.

"Hiya-aaa Je sS-s-ss--I-E!" Tisha exclaimed!

Unlike Tisha, Jessica was the last person Tahj wanted to see. "Fuck no! Jess wtf you doin here?" Tahj rose to his feet as he gently sat Louis on the couch. Focused on the movie he had no idea his mother was in the room.

Jessica dropped to her knees and crawled over to Tahj on her hands and knees. She kissed his feet and tugged on his pants.

Her hair had been scattered across her head, mascara ran down her face and her lips cracked.

"Tahj I need something I need a hit or something." Jessica begged. "You don't mis some baby?" Jessica pulled herself up and leaned on Tahj and looked him in his eyes. Parker didn't need to see his face she knew for a fact he wasn't only embarrassed but hurt. Seeing the mother of his son and his first love give up everything for drugs tore him to pieces.

"Yo Jessica get the fuck outta here?" Tahj shouted pushing her off of him causing her to stumble. Once Louis heard his mother's name he diverted his attention to the scene and screeched at his mother's presence.

"Mommmmy!" Louis shouted as he leaped off the couch into her arms. She hugged him for a second before she pushed him out the way and crawled back to Tahj. Disgusted by her mistreatment to their son he dragged her out of the house.

Parker was baffled. *"This is some crazy ass shit."*

Jessica sat outside the front door banging and screaming for 30mins before she got the picture to leave.

**

The 4-hr drive that seemed like forever left Parker in deep thought. A month ago, she would have never imagined she'd be on the run, and with someone she'd just met. Yet, here she was, fleeing to Pennsylvania.

Tahj shuffled NBA young boy albums the entire ride which kept Parker somewhat grounded even though her mind raced. Two weeks prior she quit her job so she was not only on the run but she had no income as well and from the looks of it she was shit out of luck because Tahj had $0 to his name.

Still disturbed by Tahj's distinguishing marks on his neck from the mother of his child, Parker decided to leave it be for the time being, but she took note of it.

Tahj used "wayz" to avoid tolls, so they arrived in no time. Once they crossed that line into Aliquippa, PA Parker immediately regretted fleeing town with him.

"Are you fucking kidding me right now." She thought to herself as she observed her surroundings.

"Uh, Tahj? Where we at?" Parker asked.

"Quip." He responded slyly.

Aliquppa was a city in Beaver County in PA that resembled a ghost town. There were blocks filled with crumbling houses, abandoned buildings and vacant lots overgrown with weeds. Once-bustling Franklin Avenue was still filled with traffic, but most of the cars were simply passing through town. The city's main thoroughfare, by far outnumbered the few small businesses that remain -- a caterer, a barber and a pharmacy, among a handful of others.

Tahj made a sharp right turn and glided up a steep hill to the Linmar Terrace Projects. Long, brown-brick apartment buildings, set in pleasing, orderly parallel and perpendicular lIvory, capped in green, blue, beige and white aluminum siding. The grounds were garbage-strewn, the units boarded with plywood and Graffiti had been scribbled on the walls. Residents are under police scrutiny twenty-four hours a day. The drug trade had been booming in Pennsylvania so Tahj figured why not move his operation to another state. The junkies in Pennsylvania went crazy for whatever. And when they were suffering from addiction they did anything to prevent from getting sick. Cocaine didn't kill like fentanyl which made it just as prevalent.

Parker slowly exited the car nit worrying about catching up with Tahj. She explored her surrounds and turned his nose up. They had drove hours away to a somewhat abandoned city and it alarmed her. She looked up and saw Tahj waving his hand for her to move a little faster.

"This my *friend* Parker." Tahj dryly introduced Parker to his father's side of the family and put an emphasis on friend. They said nothing and stared at her in awe. They looked her up and down and barely acknowledged her. *"Oh fuck no, they rude as hell. Dingy ass house."*

His uncle and aunt continued to stare at Parker before they broke the silence. "Well.." his uncle jumped up and stomped to the fridge, he pulled out a beer. "Want a brew?"

Parker shook her head and turned down the offer. His wife rolled her eyes. "So how are the boys Tahj?" she quickly changed the subject and diverted her focus to Tahj.

**

Parker was frustrated. She didn't know what to do, what to think let alone how to feel. She found herself head over heels for a nutcase. *"God got my neck like shit wit this one, I can't believe this shit."*

Arriving to their destination and her new temporary home, Parker let her mouth hang open.

"Nigga, is this a hair salon?" Parker questioned.

Tahj laughed and shook his head. "Naw Parker, it's apartments above the shop."

Still not content she rolled her eyes and exited the car following behind him into the building.

Tahj had got the keys from one of his older cousins. He was into real estate and this had been one of his properties so he allowed Tahj to crash for the time being.

As they descended the stairs and entered the apartment, Parker was not only disgusted but lost for words.

The apartment had looked as if it was both occupied and abandoned at the same time. Clothes were strewn all over

86

the floor, food had been splattered in the microwave, crumbs covered the counter, the smell of moldy food crept out of the refrigerator, dirty dishes were stacked in the sink, a tick layer of dust had accumulated throughout the unit as well as cobwebs; it was a horrible site to say the least.

"Now who the fuck cleaning this shit up? Cus I damn sure ain't touching shit in here. I will pay for a room fuck that."

July 2019

Parker tossed and turned on the air mattress next to Tahj. It had been a month straight since she had returned home, seen her family or talked to her friends. She had distanced herself and it was taking a toll on her. She was miserable under the circumstances she was in and what bothered her the most was that she knew it didn't have to be like this. Tahj was super distant and Parker knew from the jump he was still dealing with Sienna even with everything they had going on. She was sick and tired of sitting around being a dummy and under the horrible living conditions Tahj had her in.

"Fuck this shit." Parker spoke softly under her breath. She rolled off the floor and dressed herself. With Tahj in a deep sleep she quietly packed her belongings. Parker spotted her keys and headed to the door. She sat her bags outside and went back, gently kneeling down she kissed Tahj on the cheek and whispered. "It was all good while it last babyboy".

Parker stuffed her belongings in her car and prepared herself for the four-hour long drive. It was 3Am and she was finally headed back home.

P

A woman's only defense against falling victim to the side chick, is to be honest with herself about her needs and what she requires to be happy, and those same things in her mate.

CHAPTER 5

THE MISTRESS

"Bishop"

JOURNAL ENTRY #6

It's 11:03 p.m. and I'm texting your boyfriend. A girl who has no idea the guy she loves is currently telling me what he wants to do to me and sending pics of his eggplant emoji.

Yeah, I'm the sidechick.

I'm not a whore, although you might want to call me one. I'm not even a bitch - I'm actually a pretty nice person. I have friends and family who love me, and I don't fit the "other woman" stereotype. Ya know the one I mean - all perfect Instagram shots ft. swoon-worthy hair and curves in all the "right" places. Trust me when I say that ain't me.

I am not special. I am not prettier than you, or funnier than you, or better in bed than you. I'm not a 'slut' - I don't have one-night stands or go out with the specific aim of taking someone home. I'm not a gold digger. I'm fairly ordinary, really.

And yet, at least five of my most recent 'situationships' (and I use that term very loosely) have been with men who are… well, already in relationships.

I have friends who will never be this person. The second they hear a guy has a girlfriend, that's it - he's off limits, and they won't even entertain the idea of starting something up.

WHAT NEVER CEASES TO SURPRISE ME IS HOW MANY GUYS ARE SO WILLING TO CHEAT. These aren't 'players' that I go for. They're just normal men who love their girlfriends but, for some reason, take only the tiniest of pushes to enter the realm of infidelity.

What I want to make clear, is that I'm not sitting here cackling evilly and trying to break you up - I just seem to be missing the part of my body that should feel empathy for you.

I'm not an uncaring person. I donate to charity, I cry at long-lost-family reality shows, I can't bear to see an animal scared or in pain. But you? You aren't real to me. I haven't met you. I don't know you. And somehow that lets me do this.

It allows me to be the sidechick with no guilt, just frustration that I can't see him more, that he's not free tonight because he's playing host to your parents or taking you out for your birthday.

Perhaps it would be different if I'd been cheated on, but I haven't, so maybe I just can't comprehend the pain that comes with the discovery of infidelity.

THE REALITY THAT I WILL ALWAYS BE SECOND BEST EVENTUALLY TAKES THE SHINE OFF!

Supernatural shit aside, the reality of being the sidechick is that as exciting and as flattering as it may be at first, the realization that I will always be second best eventually takes the shine off, and things inevitably fizzle out. Then it's on to the next shiny new already-someone's-boyfriend, and so the vicious cycle continues.

Until I find my happily ever after, of course.

Therapy Session

"Bishop was just something to do when there was nothing to do." Parker sighed. Ada sat back and waited for Parker begin this short story. She kicked her feet up "He had a girlfriend the entire time." Ada raised her eyebrows in shock.

"Niggas ain't shit!" Parker shouted.

August 2019

A few weeks had gone past since Parker left Tahj exactly where he had her fucked up at. She was sick of niggas and all the bullshit that came with them. Being a side bitch was not up her alley, she wasn't the type to share, let alone a nigga at that. Parker knew for a while he wanted to be with Sienna deep down inside, but she still stuck around. She figured he'd warm up, but he never did. Although it took longer than usual, she removed herself, she found Tahj toxic in some ways; from his family to the situations, he put himself in.

She was taking some time for herself and hadn't been out in a while but that changed when her friends dragged her out.

"Okay look ima just park right here and we just goin leave it at that." Frustrated with dc parking Maelon stopped where she could, and the trio hopped out.

"Fine for me I'm just tryin get drunk." Parker added. It was a Friday night and U St. was usually jumping during the summertime on weekends. Both historic and colorful, U St. boasted some of the richest culture of the city; full of bars, restaurants and boutiques. In fact, a new bar seemingly opened up every week.

With an unparalleled music and nightlife scene, if you're looking to stay up late and have a good time, U St. is the place to be. From underground clubs to industrial chic spaces, U St. has everything in between and every option to suit your vibe.

They hit the corner of 14th and U and slide in Tropicala. In this downstairs space parties went late. They were open 7 days a week from 5pm until. Tropicana had live bands and DC's most well-known DJs.

Entering the club Parker took note of the scenery and admired the beautify in several pieces of surrealist art that adorned the walls. The floors were hand painted from Mexico and the disco lights flashed from above. Despite Parker's hate for night clubs, she needed this outing. She was the lounge type, she liked to sit back on the couch and sip champagne. She wasn't into dancing and throwing up gangs signs when the hottest song played, but tonight was different. Parker sported her Valentina Garvani Rock-studded Sneakers and paired it with a white bodycon dress from Zara she purchased at the beginning of the summer. A messy bun rested on top of her head, she wore no make up, and walked with the upmost confidence.

Future came on and she fell to her seat in their section. She was having a blast. She was six margaritas in and felt every last one. Maelon fired up the hookah and it almost put Parker down.

For the remainder of the night, she couldn't shake these peering eyes that laid on her like a hawk. Bishop stood on the opposite side of the club and kept his eyes glued to Parker; he couldn't let her out of his site. He watched as she threw shots back and moved her body to the music. He watched and watched until he couldn't take it anymore. Pushing pass the crowd he maneuvered his way to Parker. He caught her at the bar grabbing another margarita.

"Her tab on me." Bishop shouted over the music at the bartender. She acknowledged him and slid Parker her drink. Parker turned and was face to face with Bishop. More like face to stomach. Bishop was tall and dark, he had a little weight to him which was a plus for Parker.

Bishop was taller than what Parker had been used to. He was chocolate as fuck but the knot above his left eyebrow caused Parker to turn her nose up. *"Rock head ass nigga."* He had a little extra weight on him and a belly. But Parker could tell he was clean and kept himself up. Bishop was from Greenbelt MD but resided in the city.

"Thanks for the drink." Parker slurred while blushing.

Bishop laughed and shuffled from side to side, one hand in his pocket and the other with a drink. "No problem lil Ma." They stood there and gazed at one another before he broke the silence again.

"Bishop." He extended his hand.

"Oh." Parker laughed and sipped her drink. "Parker." She shook his hand.

"You should give me your number and let me take you out." He expressed.

Parker rolled her eyes and attempted to play hard to get, but she eventually gave up the number and anticipated their date.

**

Parker entered the luxury hotel in amazement. The booking process was simple, fast and discreet, the service was amazing as well. The interior design was superb, the haute couture styling with fabulous artsy features and state-of-the-art technology caught her eye instantly. The high-quality furnishings with opulent, expensive touches blew Parker away. She paid so much attention to detail and aesthetic, the room was quiet, and the air was fresh, Parker couldn't get enough of the original art on the walls either.

Parker drove around twice just to find decent parking. Tonight, she was getting laid, and she was so ready for it.

Parking enforcement took their breaks on the weekend so she parked illegally knowing she would be good.

Parker entered the hotel and surprisingly tony had been waiting for her by the elevator.

"Wassup Pretty." Bishop grabbed her and caressed her back. Parker blushed. She loved the attention and affection, every minute of it.

They got acquainted and Parker got to know more about him. Bishop was a part time music producer and a full-time drug dealer. Just like Tahj he sold coke but unlike Tahj he wasn't moving serious weight.

**

Bishop pushed Parker against the wall and started an assault on her neck where he figured he knew she liked it most. Bishop had no reservations about using my tongue, so he licked Parker up her neck to her ear. This elicited a gasp from her accompanied with her opening her legs a bit for Bishop to slide one of my own between them. he dropped kisses all over her neck and collarbones while she ground her hips into him. Bishop's hands slid from her waist to her ass, where he gripped her and lifted her higher into the wall. His hands then trailed to her breasts which were pressed into hers. Bishop squeezed each one and worked his hands towards Parker's already hard nipples. He brought his mouth to each one and used his teeth and tongue to lash them individually. When he knew Parker's nipples could get no harder, he peppered her chest with more kisses, sinking lower and lower towards her center. It appeared she had just shaved herself before she left home, leaving her legs and lower lips completely smooth. Bishop licked her inner thighs with a rough flat tongue until her hands were in his hair pushing his face where she wanted. He nipped each thigh causing her to shudder both times, then l let her have it. Bishop ambushed Parker with his tongue, alternating between ice cream licks and pointed ones. After thirty minutes of pleasure, Parker's knees almost immediately buckled as if she had been holding out for that one sole thing. Bishop let her crumble into his arms, and he waited for her to regain her strength to stand.

September 2019

It had been a month exactly since Parker started having occasional sex with Bishop. It was so amazing she couldn't give it up. He was much older and knew what to do with her which was a plus. He was consistent, dominant, and always on man time.

In the room that is twilight and shadowy, Bishop stood close enough for Parker to breathe in his scent. His arms wrap around her back and in one gentle pull their skin touched. Parker felt his hand in my hair, he loved the softness, watching it tumble as he released it. Then his hand moves down her cheekbones to her lips. That's when the kissing starts and they start to move like partners in a dance that is written in their DNA. Their bodies fit together as if they were made just for this, to fall into one another, to feel this natural rhythm. With a laugh he lifted Parker right off her feet, carrying her toward the bed, letting her fall with a soft bounce on the mattress. They lock eyes for just a moment, just enough for them to feel safe with one another. Then Bishop is all business, undoing her jeans, pulling them off, kissing from her toes upward, slowly, his hands on her legs, always just a little higher than the kisses. Parker can feel her back arch in anticipation, knowing where his fingers will soon reach. Her head rocked back against the pillow as he does, the first moan escaping her lips.

**

Parker pumped down H street in amazement. Gentrification had worked its way into the city and took over. The hood didn't look so much like the hood anymore. Being the tomboy that she was she had never really been into the whole face thing but today she was on her way to get her lashes done for the 2nd time ever. Her cousin Chenoa referred her to her own personal lash tech, Nish. She had seven years of experience in facials and specialized in lashes and eyebrows. In fact, she had been one of the most recommended lash techs in the city.

Nish lived in the Apollo which consisted of luxury upscale units. The location was convenient, her view was perfect, they offered ultra-modern amenities, 100 % safety and security. She figured it didn't get any better than that. Parker passed solid state bookstore and crossed the street to her location.

Letting her off on the 11th floor Parker sauntered to the Nish's apartment taking in the sights and features of the upscale building.

She reminisced about her sexual escapade with Bishop.

"My God that shit was amazing.." she thought to herself.

Her phone dinged twice and there were two unread messages from Bishop:

I miss you already lova
Have a good day

Parker closed the texts messages and grinned. She decided not to text back right away and give it some time. She stopped in front of Nish door and knocked twice. While waiting she looked down at her phone reading the messages in a daze as Nish opened the door.

"Hiyaaaaaa! How are you!" Nish greeted her with open arms and a huge smile.

She was cute. Nish was dark and petite. Her teeth resemble veneers, she had her orthodontists to thank for that. Her smile was bright, lit up the room and she had one dimple. Nish was the sweetest thing in the world. She was such a positive individual with so much energy. She was from Richmond VA, typical white girl trapped in a black girls body. She spoke and carried herself like Paris Hilton, but she still didn't look at herself as if she was better than anyone. She was as humble as they come for the most part.

"Ok you can go on back" Nish extended her hand as she closed the door and led Parker to the back.

Passing by Nish entertainment room her heart dropped.

"Oh dont mind my boyfriend." Nish waved him off and kept walking while Parker stopped in her tracks. Bishop sat on the sofa in awe. He had nothing to say. Parker's face was blank. She turned around and walked out the door without saying a word.

<u>October 2019</u>

"Bishop bye." Parker waved him off. He had been trying to continuously pursue Parker after she found out about Nish. "You have a whole bitch."

Parker sauntered to her car and tony followed behind her frustrated. He sighed deeply and sucked his teeth. "Parker!" He whined.

"You worried bout the wrong shit baby. Just worry about me and you." He pleaded with sad eyes.

Parker stopped and stared at him blankly. "Are you fuckin serious right now?" She paused before she began to laugh.

Bishop and swung and kicked the air from Parker's response. She was unfazed and had no problem cutting him off. She knew that if he'd do it to Nish, he do it to her, and she couldn't fade being in that predicament.

CHAPTER 6

DISTRACTION

"Emir"

P

Distractions only help you cope.
They do not resolve or help you heal from your issues.
Adding all these extra distractions to your already
overloaded plate, only creates more stress in your life.
Stress equals more anxiety, more unhappiness, and more
discontentment.
Essentially, you're doing more damage by trying to avoid or
run from the hurt you experience, than good.

Therapy Session

Ada could sense the anger and resentment all over Parker's face. "Emir was just supposed to be a distraction. I mean that's literally what it was. But.." she paused.

"But what Parker?" Ada asked.

"I got pregnant unexpectedly and unknowingly."

Ada's eyes widened. "What do you mean unknowingly? You didn't know you were expecting?"

Parker shook her head. "No. I didn't find out until three months in. This was after everything happened."

"After what? What happened before the pregnancy?" Ada wanted answers, she wanted details.

"After he carried the shit out me, he fucked me and disappeared. I only found out because of Marquee."

"How did Marquee play a part in this?" Confused and baffled at the same time, Lafonda didn't know what to think. "*This girls life is like a movie, it's never ending, it never stops with her.*"

"He tried to kill me." Parker replied calmly.

July 12th, 2020

Parker ran down the steps reciting the city girl lyrics she heard coming from outside. Kiya was sitting in the visitor's spot blasting her anthem. Parker eyes damn near fell out their sockets once she saw what Kiya had been whipping. Her words got caught in her throat. The comfort, the premium upholstery, the plush carpeting, polished wood trim and everything in between did it for Parker. This was a vehicle for the ones who liked the finer things and life, and she couldn't believe she was sitting in one at the moment.

"Bitchhhhhhhhh I miss you!" Kiya jumped across the seat and the two hugged tightly. It had been months since they had seen each other and here they were, finally reunited.

Parker and Kiya's friendship goes way back. They met at the tender age of thirteen, right before high school. With Parker always in MD, she would sneak to the city on multiple occasions and link up with her friend. As the years went by they got closer and closer and developed a bond that couldn't be broke. The two could go days, weeks, months and even years without communication but never no love lost. Besides, they always find their way back to each other.

"Ok bitch where we goin what's the move?" Kiya questioned. She wasted no time getting her plans in order.

"Girl I have no idea.." Parker fell back in her seat and waited for Kiya to put the car in drive. "I haven't been out in months."

Kiya gasped dramatically. "Oh yea that shit wit Quee, I'm sorry love. How have you been since?"

Parker shrugged her shoulders. "Girl honestly, I just been getting back to me. Learning who I am all over again, what I like to do, what makes me happy, how to be alone..."

"I get it sis.. I totally feel you and it be like that sometimes. I went thru the same shit wit Vinny." Kiya confessed.

Not wanting to talk about it no more Parker quickly changed the subject. "Yea bitch so I'm tryin' get drunk and forget about all my problems. So first we goin stop at the liquor store then we goin get some weed." Parker demanded.

"Oawwww I know exactly where we can get some weed for free." Kiya chimed in.

"Oop, me too!" Parker added.

Their eyes lit up like kids at a candy store. They were excited for their little outing.

They sped to the liquor store, grabbed 4 bottles of champagne, two packs of bamboo sheets and a large pack of funnel to last them they the weekend. Their first stop was Edgewood Commons. Parker had been more than familiar with the area being as though she had a mini fling with a certain someone from this side. She still managed to stay close to a few males, in fact they even still let her purchase her drug of choice for $0.

"Girl why the hell you got me up the Towers?" Kiya sucked her teeth and rolled her eyes. She didn't just have one, but two sneaky links that lived up the Towers and she just had a feeling she would be getting caught up fuckin wit Parker.

"Girl, relax, the niggas we bout to slide on do not know the niggas you be fuckin wit." Parker replied.

Kiya snapped her neck in Parker's direction. She didn't flinch one bit in fact she laughed.

"What's the supposed to mean bitch?"

"Exactly what I said." Parker spat back. "Pull right here and back in, there they go right dere."

A few days ago, Parker had received a text from an old friend from years ago. They stayed in touch; in fact, he was like an older brother to her. Parker used to date his drug addict cousin.

Meechie was another fling that was just for fun. Parker liked his ass until she saw his true colors and they were horrible. Meechie was not far from a mental patient. He was a true bum and still is to this very day. He introduced Parker into the world of drugs; she has seen and done some of the craziest things with him but more importantly she learned a lot of street shit from him. Parker knew about drugs and how to sell them, how to shoot guns and how to dismantle them, she also knew the ins and outs of the game; it was Meechie that put her in that shit. Their dealings were nothing but an adventure.

While she was putting the car in park Kiya noticed the crowd of dudes walking up to the car and her eyes were instantly glued on Wink. Parker exited the car and greeted everyone. She dapper majority of them up and pulled Ezzy in for a super big hug.

"Damn wassup bruh, how you?" It had been years since their last encounter. He was fresh out from doin a lil bid. He got hemmed up back in the day and decided to do his time. But now that he was back home he was better than ever, on all get money shit.

"Ain't shit sis, just tryin get some money and stay out the way. It feel good as shit to be home tho." Ezzy responded. Ezzy wasn't cute but he wasn't ugly. If it was up to Parker she wouldn't date him, he just didn't have the looks for her. His head was shaped like the egg icon from twitter. His eyes stayed low because he was constantly high, and his lips and nose were gigantic, many say he favors Rotimi from Power. He still got bitches and had money for days so his looks never mattered to him.

"Damn wassup witchu?" Wink came out the cut and crept on the crowd from the side.

"Aww wassup bruh..." Parker reached in for a hug. Wink was fine as hell. In Parker's eyes his tattoos that covered his face were a complete turn off but her friend loved it. Wink was on the shorter size, he too had a huge noggin. He was covered in graffiti from head to toe. The tattoo in between his eyes was his signature.

"That's you?" He pointed at the Benz.

Parker burst into laughter "fuck no, that's a rental nigga, iont got it like that yet."

They all laughed in unison.

"You came up here to get some gas?" Ezzy questioned.

Parker shook her head "I sure did. Y'all got some good shit?" Wink frowned his face up "fuck type question is that? We got the best shit on the north side girl." He spoke with animosity like he wanted smoke, but it was always all love with them, he was also just a really aggressive person. They pulled out several big bags of weed and began to throw them in the air and shake them around. It was all fun and games with them, but they still didn't play about their money.

"Aww damn you got somebody in the car witchu sis?" Wink being his usual nosey self, peeped his head into the car and realized Kiya had been sitting there patiently waiting while Parker chit chatted.

"Wassup witchu? Step out here Luv." Kiya did as she was told. She was more than submissive, she jumped at the opportunity. Wink was not just handsome, but he was a charmer as well and a big flirt. Parkers dropped her head with a slight grin on her face to hide her true feelings when it came to these two hooking up. She loved Wink like a brother, however, she knew he wasn't shit. Besides, she loved her best friend more and knew that she too just like herself was a hopeless romantic, so she wasn't letting things escalate any further from this day forward.

**

"Mmm he's cute, I like him." Parker rolled her eyes at Kiya comments as they dipped in and out of traffic. Kiya was in the driver seat daydreaming meanwhile Parker was on her sixth cup of champagne.

"I wonder if his Dick big." Parker spit her drink out.

"Girl you ain't goin fuck him!" She shouted.

Kiya dramatically dropped her head and made faces at Parker.

"Girl I'm having my way with these niggas and you should too!" Kiya defended herself.

"And that's all fine and dandy until you get your feelings hurt bitch." Parker replied.

"Bitch! I ain't getting my feelings involved!" Kiya popped back.

Kiya had a point but Parker still couldn't get wit having sex with someone she didn't have feelings for.

Kiya swerved around the corner heading toward Benning Rd. "And where the hell are we going ma'am?" Parker questioned. It was always some new shit wit Kiya she couldn't wait to see what she's had goin on.

"Girl just goin finessee RJ ass for some gas, that's it that's all."

Kiya made a sharp right turn and just like that they had crossed that line. River terrace was a culdesac neighborhood in Northeast. It was located on the eastern bank of the Anacostia river. Parker had never been on this end before, this place had been foreign to her although she rode pass many times. In addition to single-family row house and semi-detached houses, the neighborhood had about seventy-five rental apartments.

It was no later than 11pm, the night was still young, but Parker was beyond tipsy. The champagne had her feeling right and she couldn't wait to hit these sheets.

Kiya crept through the alley as she came to her destination. It was the middle of the summer and the niggas was out. Kiya parked the Benz and jumped out to greet the guys as they surround the car.

"Dam wassup bread and butter!" Emir yelled out.

Kiya face lit up as she recognized her longtime friend from high school. It had been years, but he was still the same as she remembered.

"Awwww hi Emir!" Kiya rushed in for a hug and they embraced each other. "How are you?"

"I'm iight" Parker filled him out from inside the car and he was by far drop dead gorgeous. His chocolate skin glistened

107

in the moonlight. His eyes were chinky but even lower because he was high.

Kiya sat out there for a few minutes and talked to the guys. Before she came back Parker took note of her painting toward the car and Emir came back in no time. Parker's heart dropped when he touched the door handle. Anxiety flooded her system; she didn't know what to do next but she maintained.

He opened the door and eased in the driver seat. His pearly white teeth instantly caught Parker's attention along with his string features.

"Wassup friend." He introduced himself and extended his hand. One foot in the car and the other out. "I'm Emir." He extended his hand.

"I'm Parker." She blushed as he held her hand and gently rubbed it. He stared at her and admired her beauty.

"Pretty Parker." He quoted. "You pretty as shit P, and I'm tryin' get to know you."

"Oh yea?" Parker played it cool.

"Damn that was fast. But damn he look good. Anddddd we did just have a conversation about having our way wit these niggas so why not."

**

Pineapple Express played on Parker's 62' and she snuggled next to Kiya in bed with a cup of ice.

"So wassup wit this nigga Emir?" Parker asked.

Kiya slowly rose up and her mouth hung open.

"Unt unt bitch not after you just gave me all that lip about Wink earlier bitch, look at you!"

"I'm just curious!" Parker laughed her out.

Although it was all fun and games Parker was still interested. "So wassup wit him?"

Kiya rolled her eyes and fell back on the bed as she began to give a summary on Emir.

"We went to collegiate together, we were real right back in school. He got some lil money now though, and as far as a girlfriend...he doesn't have one I don't think at least not that I know of. And no kids of course."

Parker shook her and crushed her ice. "Mm interesting. I gave him my number." She confessed.

"Mmm cute, I have Wink my number too." Kiya snapped back jokingly. Parker let some ice slip out her mouth and onto Kiya forehead. The two laughed for the entire night until they fell asleep.

July 16th, 2020

Parker was one with a great sense of direction. So, when Emir told her to pull up, she knew exactly where to go and was there in no time. It had only been a few days and Emir had been somewhat consistent but tonight he wanted to see her, and it was no way she was turning down the opportunity. With everything she had been going through and gone through she just wanted something good to come out of this.

Emir was your goto guy around the Terrace. He had top quality everything from guns to weed. He was your average hustler, but he also worked a 9-5. Not to mention, he was a functioning alcoholic as well.

They sat in the car four hours drinking smoking and getting to know each other.

"You know we soulmates right?" Emir expressed.

Parker laughed him out. "How you figure that?" She slowly slurred.

"You a Taurus and I'm an Pisces, we're soulmates" her replied.

**

With the door closed every pretense fell. The facade Parker and Emir showed the world melted away and they wanted was to fuck each other's brains out. Every kiss had a raw intensity - breathing fast, heart rates faster. Then before Parker knew how it happened, they were naked and their skin was moving softly together, like the fIvoryt of silk. Parker felt his hand enter from below moving fast, their tongues entwined in a kiss, and then he was inside, changing her breathing with every thrust, hearing her moans timed to his body. Then all at once he stops and kisses from her breasts to her stomach, his hands light; then he's licking and using his fingers all at once, watching her reaction, feeling how her legs move, watching her body writhe. Parker just let out moans, unable to articulate a response. In seconds Emir was on her again, fucking her harder, just long enough to intoxicate her mind before stopping again. If it's begging he wanted, he was going to have to stop long enough for her brain to start working again first.

September 5th, 2020

It had been four months since Parker's fling with Emir. She was currently pro-niggas after he hit it and quit it. He pretty much ghosted her, and she had no idea why. To make matters worse Marquee was back on her line and he wasn't letting up. He stalked her day and night, followed her wherever she went, he even shot pictures and sent them to her one night. But on this day, he decided to taunt her, which brought forth things to light.

Parkers turned her nose up as she opened the video messages Marquee had sent her. There were several girls sprawled across air mattresses on their stomachs allowing Marquee to insert himself inside of them one by one, with no protection. *"First of all, that's some nasty ass shit, and awwww bye them bitches look terrible! This shit a messs!"*

Marquee sent those videos in attempt to clear his name, but he also tried his hardest to make Parker upset. It did nothing but add icing to the cake, Parker in fact thought it was hilarious he had just become the bid.

"This fuckin aids patient, clowns ass nigga sending dick pics to men and fuckin 19yr olds raw. I hate to fuckin see it. Jesus take the wheel!"

**

Parker made her way to Kaiser and arrived in no time. She pulled into the garage and scurried into the building. She cringed as soon as she entered; It smelt like a mixture of pain? Blood, urine, vomit and tears. The mere sight of blood made Parker squirm, there were even multiple occasions where she fainted at the sight, especially if it was her own.

Parker headed to the laboratory to get her blood work done. After seeing those videos, she was not waiting, this was in fact an urgent matter for her. She was overly disgusted and embarrassed.

For months girls had been confronting her regarding Quee saying they've slept with him or have had some sort of sexual encounter with them, and Parker always felt some type of way but she left it alone. Months later the cat is out the bag and she feels like a fool.

She pulled a ticket and had a seat so she could wait for her number to be called.

"This dumbass nigga Quee won't leave me where the fuck I'm at! The audacity! And this goofy ass nigga Emir goin disappear! What type of bullshit is this? Parker it's really always something."

111

Her number popped up and she headed back. Parker sat straight up in the chair and removed her sweater. The nurse grabbed and positioned her arm and extended it. She prepped the area with an alcohol pad and applied a tourniquet 3 inches above her selected site.

"Make a fist for me sweetie." She asked nicely.

Parker balled her fist up and closed her eyes.

Quickly she gently grabbed Parker's arm and inserted the needle, instantly blood flashed through the catheter.

Once the nurse got what she needed she removed the needle from Parker's arm and applied pressure with a gauze and stuck tape on her. She labeled the appropriate tubes and Parker was good to go.

She headed home and called it a night.

**

Parker tossed and turned all night. The email notification from Kaiser alarmed her. It hadn't even been twenty-four hours, she didn't know if that was good or bad. After logging in she scrolled through her results and her heart skipped a beat. She received negative results for everything with the exception of the fact that she was 3 months pregnant.

September 18th,2020

Parker walked down Main Street alone in Baltimore. She was headed to her 9am appointment with planned parenthood for a surgical abortion procedure. She had officially hit Rock bottom. Several emotions consumed her at once. Emir was in the wind, he completely went MIA after their little shinding. He didn't respond to texts nor did he answer the phone and she had no idea why.

**

Walking into the hospital Parker could immediately smell the saturation; rather stuff warm and antiseptic, it wasn't very pleasant. She got herself signed in and was called back within fifteen minutes. The nurse gave her graham crackers, a robe, pads and water.

The doctor came back to give her numbing medication to relax the cervix and reduce the pain. The only downside Parker had an issue with is that she would be fully awake. They also directed her to take a pain reliver as well as an anti anxiety medication.

Once each pill kicked in Parker started to feel slightly woozy. *"How did you get here P? I'm so sorry, things weren't supposed to go like this.."* Parker spoke softly to herself. She quickly wiped her tears when the nurse popped her head in.

"They're ready for you." She said cheerfully.

**

Parker lie back on the cold sterile table. Draped in a garments, with her legs propped up tears slid from the corners of her eyes, she didn't know how to feel; she was feeling so much at once. The doctors and nurses attempted to make her as comfortable as possible along with the pain and numbing medications.

With short notice, they began, and Parker instantly felt pressure. The doctor stuck her with three large needles numbing the cervix. She then placed a small suction tube into Parker's uterus, the tugging sensation and cramping was unbearable; Parker screamed. The suction was used to remove the fetus and any related material. It sounded like a vacuum and took no more than 7mins. What seemed like it was forever had been over in to time, but Parker had been completely out of it.

September 29th, 2020

The emotional side effects of the termination hit Parker hard. Emir was still MIA and hadn't returned any of her calls nor did he reach out to respond about the pregnancy.

The decision to get rid of her child was not an easy one and it definitely wasn't her preferred choice. There were so many mixed feelings afterwards. That had been the worst day of her and she thought about it every single day. She felt as if her world had been falling apart.

There was a distance between her and the world. It took Parker extra effort to do anything because she was numb; she couldn't feel anything. Someone else had her remote control and constantly switched her channels without her permission. In a glass jar full of invisible goo Parker felt detached and unreachable to everyone and everything.

"*I'm so sorry..*" she sobbed. Parker lie in bed for the 9th day in the dark in the same spot.

JOURNAL ENTRY #7

Depression can be a face of someone who is smiling, telling jokes and happy, etc.

I wake up every morning, I'm alive and well, so why be depressed?

I never know how to explain depression to someone, it's different for everyone and

Comes in so many forms.

Some people describe their depression as weight that holds them down, ever-present and demanding of their time.

Others describe it as a shadow that looms in the back of your mind, always taunting and jabbing

And trying to tear you down.

Some days you have thicker skin, and some days you're drowning.

I don't think that people understand that depression is constant.

Some days it doesn't feel as heavy, it doesn't tug and pull as hard.

And other days, it knocks you down before you can even get out of bed.

Always fighting a constant battle with myself.

November 27th, 2020

The sound of gunshots blast and shattering of the windows rang out. Glass from Parker's back window flew onto her. Like a pro she bobbed and weave in and out of traffic meanwhile crazed Marquee emptied his clip in attempts to take her life. Bullets flew at Parker one by one thumping her cars exterior; he was right on her ass. Parker ducked down slightly peeking over her steering wheel and put her car in sport. The way the billets were coming she knew it was an automatic weapon. Parker quickly lifted her head and caught a glimpse of marquee reloading his clip, that' was her chance. She swerved in and out between cars and hopped off on an exit. She found a lowkey neighborhood and decided to sit for a few mins. Once she knew she was out of sight she took a deep breath.

"FUCKKKKKKKKKK! I can't get a fuckin break! I can't do this shit nomore!"

Parker shouted, kicked and screamed, she banged on the steering wheel hysterically and sobbed. Her heart beat rapidly and her hands shook.

She was tired, mentally physically and emotionally she was beat.

JOURNAL ENTRY #8

I'm not laying around the house crying or finding myself overly emotional.
I'm just mentally and emotionally incompetent at the moment.
I can't feel anything.

P

To be honest my ass don't need nomore anymore of things
that don't kill me but make me stronger. I have learned
enough lessons from love to last me a lifetime.

CHAPTER 7

<u>LUSTY ASS CONNECTION</u>

"Taahir"

Stop letting people save you for later and when it's convenient for them. The more access you give away, the less value they see.
How they goin respect you when you keep coming back after they mishandled you.
Sprinkling some pussy on a man who doesn't want you won't make him be more consistent. It will just make him conveniently come and go when he pleases so that he can get a nut off.

JOURNAL ENTRY #9

I disrespect myself every time I reach out to a nigga that doesn't care about me, every time I keep going back for sex knowing they don't value me and every time I try to be there for someone who doesn't appreciate me.

No matter how hard it might be, the love you have for yourself has to come before the love you have for anyone else.

If not, you'll be on a never ending cycle of continuously going back to someone who hurt you, because you are too afraid to let go.

Don't let your attachment be the reason you are holding yourself back.

Friends with benefits
(Phrase of a friend)
1. INFORMAL
   a. A friend with whom one has occasional and casual sexual relationship.
2. Two friends who trust each other enough to engage in sexual activity without fear of hurting the other's feelings. Ideal scenario for folk who are not interested in a serious relationship, or who do not have time for one. Not a boyfriend or girlfriend; neither party has to refrain from dating other people. Also not a word tool for a player to have sex with women he does not care about. A smart alternative to random hook-ups
3. Two friends that are sexually attracted to each other and could be great in a relationship but are not together for other reasons. How ever both do flirt and do boyfriend/girlfriend activities but both aren't officially a couple. Usually both have an unconditional care for each other and have feelings for one another but do not take it to another level because of other reasons.

Therapy Session

"I was just starting to get back to myself." Parker kicked her feet up on the ottoman and lit her next blunt; she had them pre-rolled. "Sex has made me do some dumb things Miss Lafonda." she expressed.

Ada nodded as she acknowledged Parker.

"Including continuously going back to a nigga because I got attached. That shit was so mind blowing that I couldn't give that sweet D up."

Ada laughed and shook her head. "Is that right?"

Parker nodded in agreeance. "Eventually the logical side of my brain won the battle and I cut his ass loose. Still despite knowing the relationship would never work my heart was still broken.

"Who, if I may ask?"

"Taahir, we were the best of friends, more like friends with benefits now."

"How did that happen?" Ada sat back and made herself comfortable. She was enjoying her session with Parker. Going through her police report , she wasn't as bad as they made her seem.

"Because I caught feeling and I wasn't supposed to."

P

Sex doesn't strengthen a connection.
Sex only strengthens an attachment.
It is a deep and genuine connection that will strengthen the
sex.

JOURNAL ENTRY #10

Physical touch was the only love language he activated and I continuously craved more. Some type of connection, some sort of intimacy; and that was all I could get from him. The entire foundation had been built off of intimacy. That was my requirement. His raggedy ass ain't have shit else to offer. It took a while to come to terms with this. I had to be honest with myself first...

November 2021

Parker lay outstretched on the bed, naked and exposed. The room was warm and the steady scent of candles hung in the air, the yellow glow from their flames jumps and casts shadows on the ivory walls and the white sheets she had been lying on. She stroked the smooth skin of her belly and breasts as she waited, her fingers trailed the outline of her already excited nipples.

Between her past and the recent events that had taken place within the last few weeks, Parker was yearning for any type of affection and love. She found herself back in the company of Taahir, longtime friend, now friend with benefits.

Taahir took her to the next room and as he closed the door behind him, he jumped and kissed Parker. He immediately grabbed her ass with a rough grip and started to squeeze. She turned around on her own free will and stuck her ass out while she reached for his manhood with her hand, caressing it and moaning softly.

Parker gave him the sloppiest blowjob ever, deepthroating his thick member and caressing my balls. Taahir was in ecstasy from the way she sucked. She pulled him out of her mouth and spat on his shaft and jumped on him.

Parker started riding him, bouncing in a particular way. He didn't take my eyes off of her pussy as she was there squatting on him. She started grabbing her tits and bouncing hard. Parker knew what she was doing and Taahir could tell. She would bounce hard and then slow and then hard and again slowly, giving him the chance to hold his load for some extra fun.

**

Parker was that girl who seemed to be almost addicted to love. She jumped from relationship to relationship and kept

126

taking back partners who weren't the best influence, such as Tony. Parker suffered from oxytocin dependency and the struggle was real. This specific hormone produced feelings of lust and attachment. It lights up the same parts of the brain as heroin does. Parker knew it was her pesky hormones doing what they've evolved to do. But it was a relief to her sometimes knowing these feelings weren't something she could control.

January 2021

Cars evoke autonomy and adventure: the purr of the motor responding to your touch, the way your heart rate quickens as your speed increases. Taahir picked Parker from her house and he drove me to this parking lot that was kind of empty and dark.

One thing led to another and the next Parker was on top of Taahir in the drivers seat straddling him. She came in a dress with no panties so all she had to do was lift it and she did. Taahir undid his pants and let Parker do the rest. She slid his manhood inside of her and did her thing. They didn't stop for hours. Parker was on a cloud, she couldn't get enough.

**

"Parker look Iont know any other way to say it, but we friends before anything. You can do so much better than chasing behind me. You're an amazing girl wit a good head in your shoulders. But we can't be together we AINT on that." Tony said his piece and left Parker on mute.

**

Parker dragged herself to her bedroom. She dropped her clothing where she stood and plopped in the bed with tears in her eyes. Her night went from amazing to world shattering within seconds. She laid there and decided to rewind back to 2015 when she realized she had feelings for tony.

After three years of a great friendship — of long phone calls, of making fun of each other, of seeing each other at our worst, of challenging each other to grow, of rooting for each other, of me calling him to come save me — Parker realized She was in love, and it scared the crap out of her. What scared her was that She knew. Parker knew how She felt. She knew what he meant to her. She knew if She had to choose, Shed always pick him. It was that feeling that older, more mature couples talk about, "When you know, you know."

Parker sat on her newfound knowledge of her feelings for years, hoping She could will them away. She didn't want to be in love with her best guy friend because She was afraid of losing him, but even more so, she was afraid of being rejected.

Fast forward to present day: the love that She expressed turned out to be unrequited. It was her biggest fear coming true in real time. Falling in love with someone only for it not to be reciprocated. She felt embarrassed; She felt confused; She felt exposed; She felt stupid; She was hurt.

P

When it's over and done with, you gotta stop demanding closure.
You never really get closure ever forreal from a nigga that cheated, lied to you, mistreated you, used you, manipulated you.
Stop demanding closure when it's done.
Take it for what it is and keep it pushin'.
It's not you, it's him!
Accept it for what it is.
It's time to move on from a situation when you can't grow there.
Move on. Fuck the closure.

P

To be honest, the heart will find it really difficult to be vulnerable again, to be able to trust again, to be able to speak freely without holding back again, without being open again, without being able to express everything you think again, without being the OLD YOU again.

ℙ

Forgive yourself for accepting less than you deserved, but
don't let it happen again.
If God wants you to let it go, then let it go.
Trust he has so much better in store for you.
Don't allow feeling lonely to push you into the arms of a
person who will make you miserable.
Trying to love the wrong person can cause you to lose
yourself.
Focus on loving you first and you'll never get lost.
You have to do what is truly best for you, and cutting
someone off completely may be it.

P

The 1st step to healing is acceptance. You have to accept
the true colors that people show you, no matter what you
thought they were or how they used to act. Stop
romanticizing people who are hurting you.

P

Everyone you meet isn't your potential soulmate or
someone you will fly off into the sunset with.
Some people we meet are just meant for us to learn
something from or to be our friends.

Final Therapy Session

The night was still young. Parker and Ada had spent their entire day together. She was able to make Parker feel comfortable and open up to her, I mean after all that was her job.

"Parker before I let you go, there are a few things I would like to share with you." Ada expressed.

"Sure, Parker stayed seated and didn't bother to gather her belongings; she had actually been enjoying her long chatty conversations and storytelling.

Ada sat up right her seat and leaned in toward Parker, she wanted her to know she meant every word she said.

"Parker." she paused. "You are a beautiful person, a special breed. Someone with a heart that's so strong, so sweet, so silly. Everyone will tell you to stop being how you are, this is the way of the world, to tell us how to be, but you keep on falling for people that are projects. You keep giving more of yourself than you should."

Ada paused to catch her breath and Parker wiped tears from her face as she took in Ada's words.

"It's wrong Parker.' she chastised. "You know, to try to solve everyone's problems. To try to love people who aren't yet whole. But you can't help it. You want to be the solution, the soul that makes a difference. And you are, but often at your own expense."

Ada paused once again to make sure Parker had been taking everything and indeed, she was.

"Parker, listen." Ada rose from her seat and got a spot right next to Parker on the sofa. She pulled her into her arms and consoled her as she wept. "You are the person that gives so willingly. That dives headfirst into people who cannot give the same in return. That sacrifices her own heart, her own happiness, to see a smile stretch across a broken face. You fill cracks, you mend fractures, you fit yourself into all the empty spaces. And when you fall short, you blame yourself." It's a cycle love, a cycle that leaves you the emptiest of all."

Parker sobbed and Ada let her as she rocked back and forth like a child.

"You're an amazing person Parker, I just wanted to let you know that. You are not weak because you try to solve what you can't. Foolish, maybe. But incredibly strong. But that's the thing about being a strong woman. You think you're strong enough to handle the darkest of places. You are a fixer Parker. You throw yourself into situations that aren't good for you, and most shatter you into thousands of tiny pieces. Yet, you still go forward, unafraid."

THE FINAL JOURNAL ENTRY

The beautiful thing about love is that it is forever evolving.

I used to think I had previous failed relationships, or I wasted time with men or I was crazy to think "that" was love, anything before wasn't real.

But I was wrong.

All of it was real.

A real learning experience.

I learned how to communicate, I learned what I will and will not tolerate, I learned how it felt to be hurt so I wouldn't do the same things to hurt anyone else, I learned how to be not only lovers but friends to build an everlasting partnership and team.

There's no such thing as failure on love only lessons.

I'm thankful for my past relationships because they prepared me to be ready for my soulmate.

UNLEARN AND RELEARN

"As the famous saying goes; a child is like a sponge, they take in all that they can from around them."

Although we all move based on learned behavior, the key is overstanding whether the learned behavior is healthy.

We have to unlearn the old and relearn the new.

Sometimes you can learn a lot more from a person than you planned on, it's all about your perception. Information comes in many shapes and forms, as long as your mind is open everyone can be a teacher if you can learn to decipher words and behaviors from the root. The skill to decipher behaviors will present lots of information. The key is to decipher based on reality not feelings. Behaviors are based on patterns, consideration, and information. The wisdom to understand someone's behavior and distinguish whether or not will be conducive to your growth, peace, wisdom and prosperity?

Love is a natural human craving, that's why for some in our youth we form many behaviors seeking attention from those we gain attraction to.

Oftentimes at a young age females and males go through many lustful relations. Our hearts naturally desire love, affection, reassurance, and other physical/ emotional needs that can only be provided by another human being.

With that being said it's imperative to receive those at its purest form from your family or people you grow under in your childhood. The information and care you receive in your earliest years are typically the footprints of your path created as life generates.

P

I am affirming that I am deserving of love, I will constantly
do the inner work to become a better person and I know
that the love that I have for myself isn't meant to replace
companionship.
Loving myself is enough until what is meant for me finds its
way to me, at the right time.
But until then, I won't beat myself up emotionally feeling
like my life isn't complete; everything is aligned exactly the
way it is meant to happen.

PARKER'S GEMS & PRINCIPLES

P   Real bitches wipe their face, and keep that shit movin'

P   The best revenge is no revenge. Retaliation takes time and energy; you gain nothing from it.

P   You can't force someone to see that you're a blessing. Sometimes you must let them miss out.

P   Never trust your tongue when your heart is bitter or broken. Hush until you are healed.

P   I ain't moving the same no more cause a lot of shit got to me personally and it changed me.

P   Control your emotions, doesn't mean avoid your emotions. Feel your shit, understand your shit, but don't lose your shit.

P   Bitches will see your situation and be like "*It could never be me*" you're absolutely right, it could never be you, you suck! God wouldn't put your weak ass in my position because you aren't built for it. Even in this position I'm still shitting on you, now mind ya business bitch!

P   Sometimes you just ain't bum enough for a nigga, just send his ass back to what he used to

P   Them crazy bitch days are over, been over. I'll leave a nigga alone before I ever lose my sanity.

₽ The relationship you have with yourself is the most complicated because you can't walk away from you. You have to forgive every mistake. You have to deal with every flaw. You have to find a way to love you even when you're disgusted with you.

₽ You can do whatever you want, just not with me, tuhhhh

₽ You will always be "too much" for a man who isn't enough for you.

₽ They weren't sorry when you didn't know, remember that.

₽ You're rare so people are going to fall in love with the idea of having you but most of them aren't used to rare, they're foreign to it so they'll lack the capacity to treat you as such and that's where they lose you.

₽ Sometimes you gotta blame yourself for shit you go through because you knew better.

₽ Sometimes you gotta be like "bet" and leave that shit alone.

₽ When a nigga really fuck witchu he's goin to do exactly what he's supposed to do to keep you happy and smiling. You ain't gotta guide him or ask twice.

₽ No need for revenge when you solid, your absence is goin' fuck they spirit up

₽ It is what it is, fuck what it was and what it could have been.

₽ Apology without change is manipulation.

₽ At the end of the day, I know what type of girl I am and what I bring to the table, fuck up if you want to.

₽ Can't double back, cause that's asking for another 'L'

₽ You cannot change their behavior by loving them harder.

₽ What I require, I can also provide

₽ God removes and god replaces.

₽ Can't show no emotion, that shit get you stepped on.

₽ You only exist if I want you to, this is my world.

₽ Once I see the lame in you, I can't unsee it.

₽ Money don't impress me, there's nothing you can do for me that I can't do for myself. Money only impresses broke bitches

₽ Never fight fire with fire, just watch how god handles your demons for you.

₽ Ima keep it gangsta so you never know how it affected me

₽ Stay up out your feelings that's a dangerous place to be.

BE HONEST
WITH
YOURSELF
FIRST

P

Made in the USA
Monee, IL
18 September 2021

77638789R00079